MIDLIFE IN THE FAST LANE

Sweet Mountain Witches
Paranormal Women's Fiction Novel
Book Four

CINDY STARK

www.cindystark.com

LICENSE NOTES

DISCLAIMER:

All spells in this book are purely fictional and for fun.

Visit http://www.cindystark.com for more titles and release information. Sign up for Cindy's newsletter to ensure you're always hearing the latest happenings.

ONE

I stood in front of the microwave flicking my gaze between the seconds counting down and the blue ceramic bowl inside, making sure my instant oatmeal wasn't about to bubble over the edges as it cooked. Gideon's homemade oatmeal with nuts and brown sugar was much better, but he was still snoozing in bed with my cats snuggled up against him.

Though Gideon said that he thought the chances of his younger nemesis Sauron showing up at our house had diminished, his job kept him out all hours of the night. He could say things were fine, but his actions kept me wondering.

I wished he could catch the rogue demon so that we could focus on creating a life together in our cozy cottage in the mountains. We'd yet to hike the hills of golden grass around the ski resort so that I could show him the rosy pink wild geraniums and the fiery red spikes of paintbrushes that were in bloom. I longed to wander with him in nature and explore the multitude of pristine mountain lakes and the boarded-up entrances to old silver mines instead of being afraid to leave my house without looking over my shoulder.

The sound of something skittering across the kitchen floor startled me, and I turned. A chunk of polished black hematite hit the side of my shoe and stopped. I followed the direction it had come from and found my fluffy gray cat Freya watching me with satisfaction gleaming from her green eyes.

I chuckled at her playfulness and wondered which corner of the house was now missing its protective crystal. "Good morning, Miss Freya. You're up bright and early."

She meowed, and with the toe of my shoe, I sent the hematite back to her.

The beeping of the microwave reminded me that I should be focusing on it, and my gaze jumped to the bowl inside. Globs of gooey oatmeal slithered down the sides, and I groaned. I'd been standing right in front of the microwave, and I'd still made a mess.

I shot a sideways glance at my kitty. "Look what you made me do."

Not me.

I wasn't as surprised to hear her voice inside my head as I'd once been, but it still caught me off-guard at times.

I removed a kitchen cloth from a nearby drawer and then opened the microwave. Lifting the bowl with the cloth underneath, I showed it to my kitty. "You distracted me, and look what happened."

She chuffed and batted the hematite toward me again. *Look.*

Before I could tell her that her word choice didn't make sense, Gideon strode into the kitchen carrying Old Grey with him. Our senior kitty liked to be pampered, and Gideon loved to make him happy like he did with me and Freya. My two kitties and I were spoiled by his affection.

I briefly glanced at the man who owned my heart before I continued to wipe down the sides of my bowl and inspect how much oatmeal remained in it. "You're awake awfully early."

He set Old Grey in front of the food bowl and raked his fingers through his sleep-rumpled dark hair as he approached me. "Hello, my lovely."

His voice seemed normal, but the look I found darkening his blue eyes chilled me. "What is it?"

A half-smile curved his lips, but joy didn't radiate from him. "You can read me so well."

I set the bowl down and turned more fully to him. "Tell me."

He studied me for a long moment. "I'd like it if you'd practice more defensive spells."

I swallowed the lump that had formed in my throat. "Sauron?"

He nodded, and I searched the space around us.

With his finger, he guided my gaze back to him. "Don't fear. He's not here. Not now."

Not now? "*Was he?* In Sweet Mountain Meadows? I mean other than the first time?"

He gave an almost imperceptible shake of his head. "No."

I knew there was something he wasn't saying. "But?"

Gideon released a long sigh. "He knows your name, Daisy. During a...let's call it an altercation, he asked me if I loved you."

My blood chilled. "Did you tell him?"

His snort sounded derisive. "It wasn't a matter of telling him. By asking that question, he was telling me that he already knows."

I crossed my arms in front of me in a protective gesture as my thoughts ran rampant. "What do we do?"

He tugged me into his arms, sharing his warm energy with me. "Nothing for now. Further security measures have been put in place. But I don't think it's a bad idea to prepare ourselves, just in case. Hence, buffing up your protective spells."

His words only slightly assured me. Perhaps, it was time for me to mend my relationship with the coven's high priestess and ask for her assistance. "I've been meaning to schedule a meeting with Jocelyn. I haven't spoken to her in person since that awful night when she and my mom tried their so-called intervention. She's the person most likely to know powerful offensive spells, but I'm not eager to see her again."

He grimaced at the mention of that awful scene and shook his head. "I don't want you to engage Sauron with offensive spells. I'd just like you to be able to defend yourself until I can reach you. Should the need ever arise."

I narrowed my gaze. "You keep saying 'should', but it sounds like that time is already here. And why wouldn't you want my help? I may not be the most powerful witch, but I can learn to fight back."

He gasped and placed a hand over his heart as though I'd wounded him. "Do not say such things. Don't even think them. This is not your battle, lovely Daisy, and I wouldn't survive if harm came to you."

I pushed away from him and made a disgruntled face.

He shook his head and pulled me back into his embrace. "If leaving Sweet Mountain Meadows would guarantee your safety, I'd already be gone."

I scoffed. "You're not winning any brownie points, here. First, you tell me that you don't want me to learn to fight back, and now, you're saying you'd leave me? Neither of those are okay."

Frustration darkened his features. "You can be angry if you like, but your safety is most important. I brought this to your doorstep, Daisy, and it kills me to know that."

I studied his eyes and found anguish there, which, of course, tugged on my heart. I sighed, caving to his plea. At least for the moment. "Fine. I'll strengthen my defensive spells, and I promise not to go looking for Sauron, okay?"

My statement seemed to bring him some relief. "Thank you. Now, eat your breakfast before it gets cold, and I'll drive you to work."

I slipped from his embrace and lifted the spoon resting in the bowl of cooked cereal. I tried to stir the oatmeal, but it had cooled into a firm lump. I frowned at it, and then set the bowl in the kitchen sink.

"I think I'll grab something at the shop instead. I boiled half of it over the side anyway."

He drew his brows together. "Let me cook you something."

I lifted a hand to stop him. "I really need to get out of here if I'm going to open the coffee shop on time. And I don't need a chauffeur. You said Sauron's not in town, so even if he can drive at crazy speeds like you do, he's not going to reach me in the time it takes me to get to work."

He held my gaze and shook his head firmly.

Frustration reigned, and I opened my hands in question. "Are you going to drive me every time I need to go somewhere?"

"It's dark outside, Daisy, and the road down the mountain will be deserted this time of day. These things make you more vulnerable, and I'll not have that."

I frowned, knowing he was right but not liking it. "If you're constantly driving me everywhere, how are you going to track him down?"

He curved his lips into a placating smile. "It won't be for long. Reinforcements are coming to town. I can be available whenever you need me."

I raised my brows in surprise. "Reinforcements?"

"My boss. Possibly another demon if his schedule allows."

I pointed a finger at him. "That right there proves that the situation is worse than you're letting on. Your boss wouldn't be here if everything was okay."

He took my shoulders and ran his hands up and down my arms. "This is all precautionary. Besides, it's more convenient for Antonio to operate in this area for now, and it's safer for you. As much as Sauron might desire revenge, the last thing he wants is to be captured by Antonio."

I didn't know much about the demon world's laws and consequences, but I wouldn't want to be caught doing something I shouldn't be by any of them. "What will happen to Sauron when you do catch him?"

"I'll not go into details because it's unpleasant, but he will likely cease to exist. In any form."

I swallowed at the thought and nodded. "Let me grab my purse, and we'll go. Then you should come back home and get more sleep. I'm sure the kitties won't mind a snuggle buddy."

His smile returned, full of the warmth it usually held. "I may just do that."

TWO

With Gideon's superhuman senses, the drive down the beautiful mountain canyon took half the time it normally took me. A pre-sunrise blush colored the sky as he parked his pretty black Mercedes in front of Meowkins, my cat café, and insisted on opening my door for me.

The streets of Sweet Mountain Meadows were always quiet this time of morning, and I inhaled the fresh air that still held the evening chill. Gideon held my hand as we strolled the few feet to the entrance, and he waited while I unlocked the café. I pulled open the glass door and then glanced up at him, not sure if he'd kiss me goodbye or come inside.

He lifted a shoulder and let it drop. "If the cats know I'm here and I don't stop in to say hello, they won't be happy."

I snorted a laugh. "You never fail to brighten my day."

A pleased smile curved his lips. "That's a challenge I happily accept."

I set about preparing my shop to open while Gideon headed into the Purry Parlor. When Aeri arrived twenty minutes later, and he hadn't emerged, I waited for a lull in customers before I snuck away to check on him. I opened the door leading inside and found him asleep on the couch with a half dozen cats on top of him.

I rolled my eyes and quietly approached. One by one, I lifted the rescue kitties from him. I was about to touch his face, when he reached out and gripped my wrist so tightly that I winced. His eyes flew open with his irises black as the night, and he met my gaze.

I tugged my hand to loosen his grasp. "I didn't mean to startle you."

He blinked and let go. With his expression still groggy, he sat up. "I must have fallen asleep."

I gave a light chuckle. "Yes, I would say that's exactly what happened. You should head home. You'll be more comfortable in your bed."

His eyes had faded to their normal blue color, and he gave me a sly smile as he stood. "Our bed, you mean. Would that I could take you back with me."

I slipped my arm around his waist and led him to the door of the Purry Parlor. "You need sleep, and I need to be working. Maybe, with your boss in town, you'll be able to come home at a decent hour."

He gave me several nods. "That would be a nice change, indeed."

Aeri waved to him as I walked him to the entrance. There, I stopped and gave him a quick kiss. Then I focused on his eyes. "I'm assuming you're awake enough to drive."

His smile warmed me. "Fear not. I'm awake. But I could navigate that canyon half-asleep if I needed to."

I had no doubt that he could. "Call me when you wake up again, okay?"

He planted his lips on mine. "Okay."

He called out a farewell to Aeri before he left me and headed out into the morning light.

When I returned to my spot behind the counter, Aeri lifted her brows. She fitted a white lid on a to-go cup, and I passed it to the only remaining werewolf in our town. "Have a nice day, Andre."

He smiled, and I was grateful that our past troubled encounters hadn't affected my friendship with him.

After Andre left, Aeri shot a quick glance at me. "I didn't realize Gideon was here. I thought you'd driven the Mercedes this morning."

Before I could answer, three customers walked in. I shrugged. "Long story. I'll tell you when things quiet down here."

Ten more people came and went before we reached another lull. Aeri didn't hesitate even a second to prompt me. "Well?"

I wasn't sure where I should start, but I supposed my friends deserved to hear everything because it might ultimately affect them, too. Not to mention, it was a well-known fact that a circle of witches was more powerful than one alone. "Do you remember me telling you about the rogue demon who contracted with poor Grover Jackson when he shouldn't have?"

Aeri tucked a strand of her deep brown hair behind her ear. "Yes. Solomon, right?"

"Sauron," I corrected. "He wasn't happy that Gideon had accepted Grover's soul on his behalf and then reported what Sauron had done. In fact, he's pretty angry."

The look in Aeri's dark eyes grew serious. "What does that mean?"

I sighed. "It basically means that Sauron is intent on seeking revenge before he's caught and punished for what he did. Apparently, he thinks targeting me might be a good way to get to Gideon."

Aeri sucked in a quick breath and placed a hand beneath her throat. "No, Daisy. That's...I don't even know what to say. Demons scare me."

I tried to maintain a brave expression. "I don't either. Gideon wants me to work on strengthening my defensive spells."

"That sounds like a really good idea."

I sent her a hopeful look. "Maybe the three of us could work on them together? You never know when one of us or Nicole might need to protect ourselves anyway, right?"

She gave me a solemn nod. "Yes, of course. Let's do it."

Nicole picked that moment to walk into Meowkins, which couldn't have been more perfect timing. Aeri and I waved her over to us, and then we huddled in the space between the counter and the hallway that led to the back rooms.

The second she reached us, I realized she'd been crying. "Oh, Nicole. What's wrong?"

Aeri's expression immediately turned to one of concern, too. She glanced out at the front and then wrapped an arm around Nicole and led her just inside the storage room. "Come back here, honey," she said quietly. "Where no one will see."

From my vantage point, I could keep an eye on the front door and still help console one of my best friends. I took Nicole's hand, trying to absorb some of her pain. "Are you okay?"

Nicole dropped her gaze and shook her head.

I spotted a tear as it fell from her face and landed on the top of her brown shoe. "Something with Cliff?"

It was a well-known fact that the guy she lived with was the most likely source of her unhappiness. Aeri and I had tried to get her to leave him for the longest time, but she stayed for inexplicable reasons.

"I—" Nicole began to say, but then stopped as a sob escaped her.

Aeri wrapped her in an embrace while I turned to grab a box of tissues from the storage shelf. I pulled out a few and stuffed them into Nicole's hands. "Take your time. We're here for you."

She cried for several moments before she was able to regain her composure and lift her tearstained face to us. "We had a big fight. Last night. And then again this morning."

I wished I could hex the idiot for hurting my friend. Nicole was one of the kindest, sweetest people I knew, and she deserved happiness.

"Oh, no," Aeri said. "I'm so sorry to hear that. But things will be okay. You both probably need time to cool off."

Nicole shook her head vehemently. "No. He went too far this time. I—I'm going to need help moving out my stuff."

I lifted my brows skyward. I'd been waiting for this news for a long time, and although I was heartbroken for my friend, I knew better days would be on her horizon. "Of course, Nic. Anything you need. You can come stay with me if you'd like. We have a spare bedroom."

Aeri's gaze jumped to mine, and she lifted her brows in question. "Maybe staying with me is a better idea."

Nicole glanced between us, and even in her altered state, she'd picked up on Aeri's hesitation. "Why is your place better?"

Aeri shook her head. "That's a whole other story that you don't need to hear about right now."

Nicole turned to me. "Is everything okay?"

Trust her to always put another first. I reassured her with a kind smile. "Yes. Everything's fine. But Aeri's right. Her place might be better right now."

Nicole slumped her shoulders. "I don't want to disrupt your boys and your family life."

Aeri snorted. "You mean disrupt their gaming time? They'd hardly notice that you're there."

"But you don't really have space for me."

Aeri waved away her concern. "We'll make room."

A thought popped into my head, and I gave Nicole a hopeful look. "What about staying with my mom? You know she loves you, and she'd be thrilled to have the company. She has a spare bedroom, and I'm sure you can stay for as long as you need to."

Nicole sniffed as she wiped tears from her cheeks. "You don't think she'd mind?"

I snorted. "I know she won't, but I'll check with her just to be sure."

Nicole mopped her face with the tissues and gave us a watery smile. "I'm so glad the Goddess gifted me with the best friends a girl could have."

I leaned closer to give her a hug and then spotted the purplish smudge along her jawline. I lifted my fingers toward her injury but didn't touch it. "Oh, my Goddess, Nicole. *Did Cliff hit you?*"

Whatever composure Nicole had managed broke into more sobs. "I... I..."

Aeri shook her head firmly. "There is no 'I' that should be in your response. I don't care what you might have said, he had no right to hit you. Do you have other bruises?"

She opened her hands wide but didn't answer, which was an answer in itself. Red-hot anger burned inside me. "We're calling the cops."

"No," Nicole pleaded. "Just let it be. I'll get my stuff, and he'll never have a chance to do it again."

I shook my head, not happy with her request.

Aeri did the same. "You need to report it, Nicole."

She stepped back from both of us. "I don't want to involve the police. I don't want the gossip or to have to go to court if they decide to press charges. I just want to move forward to a quiet, better life."

I released a heavy sigh and folded my arms. I wanted to see Cliff pay for what he'd done, but I didn't want to hurt my friend further, either. "At least let me talk to Corey. He'll listen if I tell him you don't want to have Cliff arrested, but this way, he can provide a police presence while we get your things. They'll make sure Cliff is out of the house while we're there, and you won't have to see him or worry that he might lose his temper again."

She didn't respond immediately and that was enough of a yes for me. "Why don't you and I go into the Purry Parlor? You know the kitties will help you feel better. I can call my mom and Corey from there while Aeri mans the counter."

Aeri nodded her agreement. "That's exactly what you need to do. Listen to your friends, Nicole. Let us help you."

She glanced between us several times and then nodded.

I exhaled in relief. If she could trust us to help her, then everything would be okay.

THREE

By the time noon rolled around, life had returned to normal. At least as much as it could with Nicole's life upended. But Corey had stopped by, spoken with her, and had promised he would support her in whatever she needed. He, of course, had also tried to convince her to press charges, but Nicole had been insistent.

But, as the Goddess intended, time would pass. Nicole's heart and bruises would heal, and her big, joyful smile would return.

With Aeri in charge of the counter and Nicole finding solace amongst the rescue kitties in the Purry Parlor, I pulled the previous day's deposit from the small safe in the backroom and headed out front to Aeri. "I'm going to take this to the bank."

She lifted her brows in concern. "Are you sure you should go out by yourself?"

I released a deep sigh because that thought had also weighed heavy on my mind. "I think I'll be okay. Gideon was mostly concerned about me being out in dark, secluded areas, like driving down the mountain in the early morning. The bank is only a short walk, and it's broad daylight with lots of people around."

The look on her face told me she wasn't convinced.

I gave her a frustrated look. "It's not as if any of us are completely helpless, Aeri. We have powers, and my top priority right now is increasing mine."

She blinked and looked away. "Then I'll tell you that you should give Jocelyn a call. She's the best person to guide you in that area."

I cringed thinking of how awkward seeing her would be. Procrastination with things that made me uncomfortable was not one of my strong suits. "I know. I'm planning on it at some point. I just need to do it, you know?"

She nodded. "I've spoken to her recently."

I lifted my brows in a challenge. "About me?"

Aeri shrugged. "She's the one who brought you up. She was concerned over how you're doing, and I reassured her that you're happy and perfectly fine."

"What did she have to say about that?"

Her expression remained unconcerned. "Not much. Only that she was happy to hear it."

I knew it was something I needed to address, but for now, I had a bank deposit to make.

Warm afternoon sun greeted me when I stepped out the door and onto the sidewalk in front of my café. The gardens along Main Street were in full bloom now with pops of color decorating my quaint hometown whose roots dated back to the 1860s when it had been a small silver mining town.

Honestly, if it got to the point where I couldn't take my daily walk, I was certain my mental health would suffer. Taking the deposit to the bank appeared like work on the outside, but it was also a chance for me to clear out any stress from the morning rush and refresh my soul. It kept me connected to the earth and to my town, and I'd be hard-pressed to ever give it up.

I reached the end of the block and paused at the corner, waiting for the stoplight to turn in my favor. We only had two in town, and those were mostly for festivals and weekends during the ski season when we had many visitors come to Sweet Mountain Meadows.

Most of the time, visitors didn't bother me. I enjoyed the extra revenue. But there was one visitor who'd become more than a pest, and the sooner Gideon apprehended him, the better.

Something akin to a spider crawling across my skin sent a shiver through me, and I cast a cautious glance around, searching for the source of the warning.

Everything appeared normal. In fact, I knew most of the people that I saw. I couldn't spot any dark auras amongst the others, and nothing seemed amiss. The logical part of my brain kicked in, forcing me to consider that the emotional side might be frightening me unnecessarily, like what happened when I'd watch a scary movie.

I filled my lungs with fresh air, opened my senses fully, and exhaled. There were no dark beings in my vicinity. Everything was fine, which reminded me that I needed to remember balance in all things. There was nothing wrong with being cautious, but I didn't want to take it too far, either.

The light changed, and I stepped off the sidewalk onto the crosswalk. As I did, a police cruiser entered the intersection, traveling the opposite direction, and it took me a moment to realize Corey was behind the wheel.

Our gazes connected, and I was about to lift my hand in greeting when he quickly glanced away. His odd demeanor set off my internal alarm, and I stopped in the middle of the crosswalk so that I could watch where he went. His brake lights flared red when he reached Meowkins, and my heart sank.

I quickly abandoned the idea of taking the deposit to the bank and hurried back toward the café. After Corey exited his car, he glanced in my direction, but once again, he didn't acknowledge my presence. That's all it took to confirm that he was in officer mode and not functioning as a charming friend.

I shifted my pace from a fast walk to running, which left me mildly winded by the time I reached Meowkins. I jerked open the door and immediately scanned the café. A few customers sat at tables, and Aeri was behind the counter, but I saw no sign of Corey.

Aeri met my gaze with a wide-eyed one of her own and tilted her head toward the Purry Parlor.

I didn't know what had happened, but everything inside me said it wasn't good. I dropped the bank deposit bag on the counter in front of Aeri. "Will you put that away for me?"

Without waiting for her response, I strode to the Parlor and pulled open the door. Nicole stood in front of Corey with her face in her hands. Both held their bodies rigid enough to rival the mountains towering over the town. "What's going on here?"

Nicole lifted her gaze and glanced at me long enough that I could see the tears streaming down her cheeks. Then she focused on Corey.

He jerked his gaze to me. "You need to leave, Daisy."

I gasped. "I don't think so. You're in my building, and you've obviously said something to upset my friend."

"This is official police business."

I shook my head, letting him know that I wasn't going anywhere.

He huffed and focused on my friend. "Nicole Santoro, you're wanted for questioning for the murder of Cliff Harrison. You need to come with me."

The air flew from my lungs. *"Cliff's dead?"*

Nicole clenched her jaw. "I didn't do it."

I couldn't have heard them correctly. *"Oh, my Goddess. What?* You think Nicole killed him?"

Corey didn't acknowledge me for even a second. Instead, he took a step closer to Nicole. "You need to come with me to the station."

Something dark and powerful surged inside my sweet friend, an emotion I'd never witnessed before. "I didn't kill him, and I'm not going with you. If I do, everyone will think I'm guilty."

The whole world seemed to have lost its senses. "No, no, no. This isn't right. Nicole could never do such a thing. Can't you take her statement here?"

Corey ignored me and reached behind him, pulling out a pair of shiny silver handcuffs. "Let's not do this the hard way, Nicole. You have to come with me."

When he took a step toward her, the entire energy in the room seemed to be sucked toward her, and the next thing I knew, Corey flew backward and landed hard on a pile of cat toys that squeaked and rattled in objection.

I froze, stunned by what had happened.

Corey was back on his feet in a second. He pressed the mic on his uniform. "This is Sergeant Shelton requesting assistance at Meowkins Café." He paused as the dispatcher replied, and then he responded in the affirmative.

I widened my eyes in horror. "Did you just call for backup? *On us?*"

He lifted his ball cap and righted it on his head. "Only from the station. Don't make me ask for magical help, Nicole. You've already taken things from bad to worse. Don't do anything else stupid."

At that point, the enormity of the situation hit me. One of my dearest friends was suspected of committing murder, and worse, she'd just assaulted a police officer. I didn't have time to piece everything together, but I knew I needed to shift my focus from Corey to Nicole if I was going to be of any help.

Pieces of my heart fell to the wayside as I stepped closer to her. I squashed the anger and indignity, praying that my emotions hadn't added to her reaction, and I lifted a calming hand. "Nicole, look at me."

She turned her gaze to me and anguish poured from her, flooding the area around us. I reached for her hand, and she let me take it. From there, it was only another step until I could fold her in my embrace. She fell apart then, emotionally and physically, and it took all my strength to keep her standing upright. "Come," I urged. "Let's sit."

As we made our way to the couch, I cast a look at Corey. His anger had simmered to irritation, but I sensed it wouldn't take much to rekindle it. "Let me talk to her, okay?"

"I'll give you until backup arrives."

I wanted to be upset with him, but I knew he was only doing his job.

Seated on the couch, I held Nicole while she purged angst from her soul. When her sobs had quieted enough, I gently stroked her dark curls that seemed to have grown wilder in her despair. "I know you didn't kill Cliff, okay? So, try to calm down if you can. I'm sure it was a shock to hear the news."

She nodded but didn't speak.

I exhaled some of the trepidation that had built inside me. "Calmer minds will prevail here, Nic. I know you didn't mean to lash out at Corey, and you need to remember that he's only doing his job."

Her anxiety spiked, and she lifted her gaze to me. "I didn't kill Cliff."

I squeezed her tighter. "I know. I know. But there's a process here. A process of law, and we must follow it, okay? If they need to question you at the station, then just go. That's the best and fastest way to clear your name, and I'll be there with you."

She remained silent for some moments though I could still sense the desolation rolling through her. Then she lifted her gaze to me and blinked several times.

I wiped tears from beneath her cheeks. "It's okay. You're okay."

Her expression crumpled, but she turned to Corey and nodded.

He shook his head in dismay. "Are you ready to go?"

She stood, dropped her gaze to the floor, and held limp wrists out to him.

He strode closer, but instead of cuffing her, he put a thumb under her chin and forced her to look at him. "I don't want to cuff you, Nicole. If you come willingly, it won't be necessary."

She nodded again and then held a hand out to me. When I took it, she wrapped fingers that were desperate with fear around my hand.

I didn't complain about the pressure but squeezed her back instead. I lifted my gaze to Corey. "Can I ride with you?"

He hesitated and then sighed. "Yeah."

As we walked out the door of the Parlor, two uniformed officers burst in through the front door. Corey held up a hand. "The situation's under control. Thanks."

I turned to Aeri who regarded me with a terrified expression. "I'm going with Nicole, and I'll talk to you later."

She nodded. When we reached the front door, she called out. "Text me."

I lifted a hand to show that I'd heard her, and then I steeled myself for what the rest of the day might bring for my friend.

FOUR

A s it turned out, supporting Nicole on the short drive to the police station was all the help I could give her. Corey had ushered me into the reception area and then escorted Nicole through the door leading to the rest of the police department. The receptionist who'd been so friendly and helpful to me on other visits had refused all my requests to see Nicole or Corey, and the door that had been opened easily for me in the past had become an impenetrable barrier.

I sent several messages to Aeri, trying to answer her questions, but the reality was that I didn't know much except that Cliff was dead and Nicole was a suspect. On the bright side, Aeri let me know that Sailor Strickland had dropped by and had volunteered to be our unofficial manager of the Purry Parlor for the rest of the day. At least one thing was working in my favor.

The final time that I asked the receptionist if Corey could see me, she passed along a message from him, telling me to go home because there was nothing that I could do for the time being. My years on Earth had taught me to recognize which battles to fight and when to regroup. Resigned, I headed out the door, already conjuring other ways I might be able to help.

The day seemed much like it had earlier when I'd attempted to go to the bank, except that the sun now played in the western sky. Cars drove past, and people entered and left buildings acting as if they hadn't a care in the world. I sincerely hoped they didn't, and I wished that I was one of them.

Halfway back to Meowkins, the odd sensation that I'd experienced earlier reappeared. A shiver raced through me, and I glanced over my shoulder. When I found no one nearby, I stopped to get a better feel for my surroundings.

After several moments of trying to locate the source of my unease, nothing and no one seemed suspect, so I began walking again. Meowkins, and therefore safety, was in sight. If I needed to, I could run the distance in less than a minute thanks to the cardio training Nicole had forced me into at the Expanding Universe exercise studio.

I calmed my worries, reminded myself to ask Gideon to help smudge me of negative energy the next time we had an opportunity, and then I continued at a pace that wouldn't add to my internal fears.

I'd only made it a few steps when the strange perception hit me harder than it had before, stopping me completely in my tracks. My pulse thrummed in my head, and my skin grew clammy. I swallowed as I glanced wildly around me, not seeing any sort of a threat.

But it was there.

I knew it with every fiber of my being. And it had to be Sauron.

There was no one besides possibly Gideon who could accomplish such a feat, and he wouldn't. Unless the fear wasn't real, and someone had cast a hex on me. Though I couldn't think of anyone who'd do such a thing.

Except maybe Vivian if she was truly that desperate to get me out of the picture so that she could have Gideon.

The feeling grew stronger, and nausea followed closely behind. Though there was no physical entity that I could see, my body forced me to take a few steps backward. And my physical reaction lessened. Thank the Goddess.

I retreated a few more steps and realized that whatever it was, it didn't want me to go back to Meowkins.

As I pulled the phone from my pocket, I kept my gaze hyper-focused on my surroundings, looking for something, anything to alert me. With a quick glance at the phone's screen, I tapped on Gideon's phone number.

He answered before I heard it ring. "I'm coming."

His response drilled terror straight into my heart. "Is it...is it Sauron?"

"Yes, Daisy. He's close."

My insides quivered as I peered everywhere around me. It was then that I noticed that even though it was broad daylight, there wasn't a single person near me. It was as though the entire block had been cleared. "I think he's here now. Very close."

Gideon released a string of unintelligible words that sounded like curses. Then he spoke to me in a calm voice. "If you see him, *run*. Don't let him touch you. I'll be there momentarily."

The sound of his car's powerful engine roared in the background, and I tried to reassure myself that I'd be safe. Gideon would make sure that I was.

Then I slammed into something unseen and a wave of intense revulsion overtook me. I had no choice but to empty my stomach into a nearby garbage can. Whatever had me in its sights, whether it was Sauron or something he'd created, it blocked my path once again. Cold crept over me, and I barely had time to wipe my mouth before I switched directions and took off running toward Meowkins.

"Daisy? What's happening?"

Exertion made it hard to breathe, and I couldn't focus on the conversation. I could only think that I needed to remain a moving target until Gideon arrived. "Please hurry."

I made it half a block before I hit that stomach-churning wall again. "Who are you?" I hollered into the space around me.

No one responded, but when I exhaled, my breath condensed in front of me as though it was winter. I had no choice but to turn and run the opposite way again.

Gideon's voice yelled from my phone, but I couldn't answer.

I didn't get far down the sidewalk this time before another attack stopped me. My teeth began to chatter from the chill, and I would have thrown up a second time if I'd had anything left in my stomach. "Leave me alone!"

"Daisy?"

The sound of my mother's voice nearly ended me. I frantically looked around until I spotted her and Mona at the crosswalk that separated my block from hers. I widened my eyes and shook my head repeatedly, warning her not to come. "Go back. *Go back!*"

The two older ladies stopped abruptly, and shock painted their expressions.

Even with Mona's help, my mother would be no match for Sauron's strength.

Though it would take me off Main Street and make it harder for Gideon to reach me, I turned and ran into a passageway between two of the old brick buildings. I held the phone to my ear. "I'm not on Main Street any longer. Headed east. My mom. She's here. I had to lead him away. Find me on First Street."

"I know exactly where you are. You don't have to say."

I gasped in relief and drew another breath. *"I need you."*

When Gideon didn't reply, my fear intensified. I glanced at the screen and found it completely black. "No, no," I whispered.

I switched my gaze between the narrow street ahead and my phone, constantly making sure the path was clear while I pushed the button to turn on the screen. Nothing happened. The connection between Gideon and me was completely dead.

The terror of my situation threatened to undermine my ability to think. Unholy thoughts raced through my mind, tripping over each other, leaving me dizzy and confused. The force of what I was up against was powerful.

But then a quiet voice in my head whispered above the clamor, telling me I was stronger.

I wasn't sure I believed it, but I grabbed the lifeline anyway. I could do this. I could hold on longer.

I'd almost made it to the end of the alleyway. Gideon said he could find me wherever I was. I could do this.

My mom was safely behind me somewhere, and Sauron was...

Where was he?

Inescapable panic flooded me. Was he going after my mom after all? Had I not led him away?

Then the familiar nausea hit, and I knew where he was. Directly in front of me. An absurd mixture of gratitude and fear twisted inside me.

But that was cut horribly short when I realized the fatal flaw in my plan because I now had to head back in the opposite direction, toward my mom, and possibly put her in danger again.

Goddess, help me.

Evil, ethereal laughter encircled me, and I tried to sense the direction it came from. Behind me? In front? Overhead?

I had no doubt that Sauron toyed with me, and I'd bet my best crystals that he took great pleasure from the act.

Again, I smacked the invisible wall, grunted from my body's response to it, and turned. Unfortunately, I only took ten steps before I was forced to turn again. Then seven. Then three.

Before I could formulate a plan, the presence descended upon me. I had nowhere left to run. I flattened against a brick wall as the form of a man began to take shape. The entity that I feared was Sauron was there, right in front of me, and I had nowhere to go. There was nowhere that he couldn't reach me except my home and Meowkins, and I couldn't get to either of those places.

I rapidly whispered my strongest protection spell as if it was a prayer, and then I added one of those, too. The energy from the spell seemed to push him backward, but not for long.

Something that reminded me of a sparkler circled the space I'd secured with my spell. Then it fizzled to nothing along with my protected area, proving the futility of my magic against Sauron.

The necklace that my mother and Jocelyn had charmed to alert me of someone trying to steal my soul burned the valley between my breasts, and I gasped in pain.

Sauron, now fully formed, advanced toward me with a cocky gait, erasing the little space between us. "You have nothing to fear from me, Daisy."

His longer blond hair with bangs swept to the side gave him a boyish look, but his fully black eyes were a window to his soul. Or lack of one, perhaps. His voice was refined like Gideon's, but it wasn't warm and loving. Instead, the chill of it sliced like a monster's claw.

Though I kept my gaze pinned on him, I dropped my hand into my bag, furiously searching for my magical pepper spray. I doubted it would stop him, but maybe it could buy me time. "If I had nothing to fear, you wouldn't have trapped me here."

He gave a casual shrug. "I merely wanted to speak to you, and this was the only way to make that happen."

I highly doubted that. "I don't have anything to say to you."

A crafty smile curved his lips, and he sighed. "I thought *you* of all people wouldn't be afraid to talk to a demon. I only want to ask a favor."

Instinct forced me to make another run for it, but he was on the opposite side of me in an instant. "Please, just a moment of your time."

I stumbled backward several steps, fully aware that the minute that he'd asked for might be my last moment alive. I needed Gideon *now*.

FIVE

I wasn't sure where the clarity came from, but a plan formulated in my head. Without questioning its ability to work, I made another attempt to run hoping to upset Sauron's cool and calculated demeanor. When he blocked my path like I knew he would, I lifted the pepper spray and pressed the button. A stream of liquid spurted forth, creating a misty haze between us.

Sauron cursed and swiped at his eyes with quick fingers.

Satisfaction burst inside me, and I capitalized on the brief reprieve. I swiveled and ran like the devil chased me. Which he sort of did.

I made it to the end of the alley and emerged onto the empty sidewalk along Main Street. The fact that I had done so, unhindered, shocked me to the core. It occurred to me that my magic might be stronger than I'd originally thought. I'd never needed to use the pepper spray before, so I'd had no way to test its potency.

But that was something to ponder for another time. I might have waylaid Sauron, but I'd by no means incapacitated him. At least my mother and Mona had vacated the vicinity.

I didn't slow as I turned toward Meowkins, the closest sanctuary. When the sound of a powerful engine grew louder, I dared a glance over my shoulder and spotted Gideon's black Mercedes barreling toward me.

Tires screeched as he stopped in the middle of the street, sending the smell of burning rubber into the air. He flung open his door and raced toward me.

Tears of relief flooded my eyes.

He gripped me by the upper arms and searched my face. "Are you hurt?"

I shook my head and pointed to the passageway between the two brick buildings. "He's in that alley. At least, he was."

He pushed me toward the street before he hurried away. "Get in my car," he called. "Stay there."

I jumped in through the open driver's side door and pulled it shut behind me. Then I locked the doors for good measure, though I doubted they would hinder Sauron unless Gideon had magically protected his car. Which, knowing him, he probably had.

The sound of silence and Gideon's warm energy filled the inside of his car, and I inhaled air in big gulps. I was safe. I prayed to the Goddess that Gideon would be as well.

I closed my eyes for a second, focusing on slowing my heart rate. That was until a loud yowling from the backseat startled me right back into fight or flight mode. I jerked my head around as a ball of gray fur jumped onto the center console.

"Freya," I said breathlessly.

What were you thinking?

Her words stunned me, and I blinked. The last thing I'd expected was to be chastised by my cat. Especially when Freya had barely been able to put words together that morning. "Excuse me, but I didn't have anything to do with this. I'm the victim here."

She chuffed in disappointment. *Gideon said wait.*

Stunned, I dropped my jaw. First because she was taking Gideon's side, and second because she did not know how to communicate this well.

Before I could comment on either of those things, the ringing of my phone caused any remaining solace that I'd found to evaporate. I placed my hand on my chest. If I didn't settle my nerves, I'd do myself in with a heart attack.

At least my phone was working again. I pulled it out and found my mom's face and name on the screen. I had to answer, but if she discovered how upset I was, she'd never give Gideon a chance.

I did my best to swallow my emotions and then tapped the answer button. "Mum. Are you okay? Are you and Mona in the café?"

"Great Goddess, Daisy. What the devil is going on?"

For whatever reason, the irritation in her voice brought me great relief. I swallowed my nerves. "It's...it's a lot to explain. I can't do it over the phone. Just please, stay where you are for right now, okay? I need you to be safe there."

"We're safe, but what about you? The necklace went off," she said in an accusing tone. "You can't deny what Gideon has done. It's time for you to come home."

"No, Mum. No. It wasn't Gideon. He's the one who saved me. He's going after the demon right now."

Silence echoed between us like a deafening bell. I needed to make her understand, but I didn't know how. Not until the adrenaline raging through me faded and I had time to think. "Please, Mum. Just please trust me, okay? I'm safe. You're safe. I do need to talk to you, but I need a little time first."

A heavy sigh echoed from my phone. "Where are you? Mona and I will come get you."

Her insistence that she protect me while I was trying to do the same for her frustrated me. "No. You need to stay where you are. I'll be there shortly."

"I think you're in over your head."

I had no doubt that she was right, but now wasn't the time to argue it. "I need you to stay there. If you come looking for me, it will only make things worse."

She hesitated for a long moment. "Fine. Just know that I'm not okay with any of this."

It was a reprieve, and that's all I needed. "Thanks, Mum. If you need anything, Aeri will give you and Mona whatever you want."

She snorted. "What I want is to talk to you. You have me worried sick, and I know Aeri feels the same."

Guilt rushed over me like dark clouds coming across the mountains.

Someone tapped on the driver's window, and I jumped. I turned to see the man-stealing witch Vivian Fowler on the opposite side of the tinted window. "Everything is fine, Mum. Gotta go. Talk to you soon."

I hung up without waiting for her response. The Goddess knew I didn't have time to argue with her. I glanced at Vivian and lowered the tinted window a few inches.

She seemed surprised to see me. "Oh."

I narrowed my gaze. "Did you need something?"

She glanced around her and then thumbed over her shoulder. "You're blocking traffic."

I flicked my gaze to the rearview mirror and spotted several cars waiting behind Gideon's. "Oh, sorry. I didn't realize."

She gave me a smug smile, turned on her high heels, and strode toward the sidewalk. She wasn't even one of the people that I'd inconvenienced. I studied her, knowing she was up to something, and then realized she'd expected to find Gideon behind the wheel.

Obviously, I needed to keep closer tabs on her. But first, I needed to move his Mercedes.

Gideon had left the engine running, so I shifted the car into gear. I cranked the steering wheel to turn it in the opposite direction and pulled up alongside the curb. I couldn't bring myself to look at the drivers of the other cars, not wanting to see the annoyed expressions on their faces. Honestly, if any of them had seen me running back and forth on the sidewalk, acting like a crazy person, and then jumping into a car parked in the middle of the road, they might try to have me locked away where I couldn't hurt anyone.

When Gideon emerged from the alleyway seconds later, I blew out a weighted breath. Instead of heading to the driver's side of the car, he strode straight toward the passenger seat. He climbed in and pulled the door closed behind him. His breaths came heavy, so I gave him a moment to recover.

When he looked at me, the black in his irises concealed most of his blue eyes. "He got away."

His words left me with a chill. One that soon encompassed the whole of me, knowing that Sauron was still out there, still a threat to me and my loved ones. "What happened?"

Gideon scrubbed his jaw. "He must have sensed me because he was long gone. It'll be easier when Antonio is here and there's two of us to trap him. Where's your mother now?"

His concern for her tugged on my heart. "Meowkins. I knew it was an area you'd protected, so I sent her and Mona there."

He patted my thigh and nodded. "Good thinking. They're safe there. Though once they leave, things might be different. I think Mona's far enough removed from you that I don't expect her to be in any danger, but it's best if we take precautions for them both."

I placed my hand over my heart, sick at the thought. "You think he'll go after them, too?"

"I can't be certain." He pulled my hand from my chest and folded it between his. "I'm so sorry for all of this."

The despair on his face made me want to cry. "No. No. You had no idea this would happen. It's partly my fault, too. If you hadn't accompanied me to Grover Jackson's house, Sauron wouldn't be bent on revenge for taking what was his."

He shook his head. "That happened after I dragged you into my world of darkness. If I would have left you alone, we wouldn't be here."

I gave him a sad frown. "But you've brought so much light into my life, Gideon. You have to know I wouldn't change things."

He squeezed my hand but didn't seem convinced. "Let's get your mother home where she'll be safe and comfortable."

SIX

I drove us to Meowkins and parked. Before I could exit the car, Freya jumped onto my lap. *I'm coming.*

I nodded and pulled her into my arms before I lifted my gaze to Gideon. "What are you doing with her to make her talk like this? This morning, she was nowhere near this advanced."

He shook his head. "Nothing recently. She must be practicing on her own."

I lowered my gaze to her beautiful green eyes. "I don't know. It always seems like she does better when you're around."

Freya tilted her head to the side. *It's you.*

I leaned back, surprised. "Me?"

Gideon opened his door. "That's what she said."

I studied Freya's eyes while I waited for Gideon to get my door. Me? I did sense that our connection was stronger, but I really hadn't done anything different with her.

When Gideon and I approached Meowkins, I noticed my mother and Mona seated at the barstools in front of the big picture window, watching from the best view currently available to them. Once inside, I found a line of customers six deep waiting for Aeri to help them. She glanced up, and I mouthed an apology. She returned my gesture with a look that said she needed answers and soon.

I nodded, letting her know that I understood.

My mom turned to me as we neared and slid from her stool, and I regretted that the worry I'd caused her had deepened the lines near her eyes. Her gait was stiff as she walked toward us. Mona, still lithe and limber in her old age, hopped from her stool and followed behind.

My mom flicked an unpleasant look at Gideon before she focused on me. "It's not good for an old lady's heart to watch her daughter race up and down the street like a mad woman. I'm sure anyone who saw you thought you'd lost your mind."

I didn't bother to mention that Sauron had somehow managed to clear the streets of onlookers. "I'm sorry that you witnessed me in a frightened state."

She huffed. "I don't mean to make this about me. I could see that you were terrified. If I would have known what was happening, I would have intervened."

Mona nodded enthusiastically. "Same for me. We old broads carry a fair amount of power, you know?"

The concern in both of their eyes caused me to release a heavy sigh. "Thank you, but it's better that you did nothing."

My mom's gaze slid in an accusatory way to Gideon.

He dipped his head. "I'll apologize to both of you. I'm sorry I wasn't here when things got out of hand."

My mom didn't look away. "Why weren't you?"

I gasped. "Mum, please."

She lifted her hand, palm outward. "No. I want to know. You've involved my daughter in demon affairs without the ability to protect her."

I sensed the heat building inside Gideon, but it didn't show in his expression. "You'll never know how deeply sorry I am for that. Though I take exception to not having the ability to protect Daisy. I underestimated my opponent, but I guarantee that will not happen again."

She shook her head in dismay and shifted her gaze to me. "You can't trust a demon."

Before I could respond, Gideon did. "That's like saying you can't trust a witch, when we all know that some witches are trustworthy while others aren't. You can't judge us all by one's actions."

She opened her mouth and then closed it. A few seconds passed before she spoke again. "I suppose that's true."

His mood seemed to lighten, and he nodded. "I hope you'll allow me to show you that I'm one of the good guys."

She pursed her lips and then studied me.

I gave her a hopeful smile. "I love him, Mum. Please give him a chance."

Mona nudged my mother. "I'll give him a chance. Look how cute he is."

Gideon lifted his brows and graced Mona with a warm smile.

My mom turned to her friend. "Cute doesn't equate to being a decent person."

She shrugged. "No, but it doesn't hurt. Besides, can't you see into his heart? He loves your girl, and I believe he'll do his best to protect her."

My mother glanced between us. "It's not like I have a say anyway. She's been on her own for twenty years. She won't listen to me now."

"So, that's a yes?" I asked my mother.

She hesitated for several uncomfortable moments and then sighed. "Maybe."

I sent her a grateful smile, knowing that if she only gave him the smallest chance, it would be enough. "Thank you. For now, we should get you home where you're safe. Who drove?"

They glanced at each other before my mother answered. "Mona's sister dropped us off at the post office. She'll pick us up after she's finished at the grocery store."

I shook my head. "It's best if we take you home, just in case. Gideon will be able to protect your houses so that you're safe while you're inside. It will protect Nicole, too, while she's staying with you."

Mona snorted. "Uh...you might want to let my sister and me take care of our own. Drop me off at your mom's, and I'll have Geraldine pick me up there. Best if you keep a low profile for now, Gideon. There must not be many in town who know you're a demon because that rumor hasn't ignited yet. The longer you can keep that from happening, the better. Who knows what these crazy witches will do?"

He dipped his head toward Mona. "Thank you for thinking of me. If you change your mind, just let Daisy know."

My mom folded her arms. "I'm capable of taking care of myself, too."

I stepped forward and linked my arm through hers. "This isn't to cast aspersions on the strength of your powers. It's extra protection, okay? You need to let Gideon get you home safely. Both of you. Then you can cast whatever spells you think are necessary."

Gideon moved closer to me. "It's not for forever, Mrs. Summers. Just until we get this matter under control."

My mom lifted her brows, her eyes flashing with irritation. "We? Is Daisy helping you with this rogue demon then?"

He was quick to shake his head. "No. Daisy also needs to remain where she's safe."

Which didn't sit well with me. Yes, Sauron scared me more than anything ever had in my life, but I wanted the opportunity to learn more about his power and ways to counteract it. Not hide in a corner.

My mother snorted. "Then by 'we', do you mean you and your pinky finger?"

Gideon's smile returned. "No, ma'am. My boss will be here before sundown, and we'll work in tandem. Witches aren't the only ones whose strength increases when combined with others."

She flicked her hand in a dramatic gesture. "Oh, great. Another demon's coming to town. There goes the neighborhood."

A laugh burst from Mona, and she nudged my mom. "Sakes alive, Bridget. You can be funny when you want to."

My mother scowled. "I wasn't making a joke."

The sooner we got her home, the better for everyone. "Give me a second to talk to Aeri, and then we should go."

I hated giving Aeri only the briefest details, but time didn't allow for more. I promised I would call the second I was home and we could discuss murder, demons, and how to help our best friend.

When we reached the car, I thought Gideon was only opening my door for me, but he surprised me when all three passenger doors opened at once. I lifted my gaze to him before I climbed in holding Freya, but he only smiled.

"A gentleman, too," Mona said with excitement.

"Show off," my mom muttered beneath her breath once she was seated inside. She pulled her door closed before Gideon could get it for her. Although she couldn't see me, I still rolled my eyes as Gideon sat in the driver's seat and closed his door.

"Stop being a grumpy old witch," Mona said in what she probably thought was a whisper.

"Stop telling me what to do," my mom retorted. "You wouldn't be so happy if it was *your* daughter dating a demon."

Mona snorted. "I would if he looked like him."

I met Gideon's gaze, and he smiled. It was obvious he liked Mona and she liked him. Not to mention, Mona's appreciation could only help my case.

Halfway to my mom's house, Mona started to complain. "I thought this fancy beast would go faster."

Gideon chuckled. "You want to go faster?"

I turned to him in alarm and shook my head. Driving like a crazed demon would not impress my mom.

Amusement sparkled in his eyes. He lifted his hand and gestured with his thumb and forefinger an inch apart, indicating a small amount.

I sent him a look that said whatever happened would be all on him.

He grinned. "Hang on to your hats, ladies."

"I'm not wearing a—"

My mom didn't get a chance to finish her sentence before the car's engine dug in deep and shot us forward fast enough that I felt it in my stomach. Mona chortled with joy, making me laugh, too.

I didn't bother looking back to check my mom's expression.

We arrived at my mother's house in record time, and Gideon parked along the curb. I could hear the click of door levers when the older witches in the backseat tried to exit the car, but Gideon held up a hand. "Give me a moment, please."

He stepped out of the car and closed the door behind him. I watched through the windshield as he focused in each direction, and then all our doors opened for us. "All clear."

I carried Freya as we followed in a line behind my mom to her front porch. She unlocked her door, paused to let Mona enter, and then turned to Gideon and me, blocking our entrance. "Do what you must out here, but I won't have any demon magic in my house."

I was about to voice my outrage when Gideon dipped his head. "Understood. Do cast your best protective spells though. Daisy can help me with outside ones."

My mother gave what might have been an agreeable nod and closed the door between us.

SEVEN

With Mona and my mom likely casting protective spells in her house, I turned to Gideon with an apologetic smile. "I'm sorry. You've done nothing to deserve the way she's treating you."

He drew his thumb along the crease between my cheek and my mouth. "Except be your demon lover."

His response brought a smile to my face. "I guess there is that."

He placed a quick kiss on my lips. "With your mom safe, let's get this done so that I can get back to *other* issues."

Other, meaning Sauron, but I had no desire to speak his name, either. "What exactly are we going to do?"

His eyes sparkled with interest. "There's an incantation, a spell if you will, that marks this house as mine. No other demon may enter without my permission."

I widened my eyes. "Is that what you've done at our cottage? At Meowkins? Marked them as yours?"

He nodded, and his response left me with a shiver. "Can you mark people as yours as well?" I asked.

He gave me a gentle smile. "Not in the way that you're thinking. It's not such a trivial matter as with objects. People and animals, those with souls, must give their consent."

Obviously, I had a lot to learn about demon customs and rules. "Animals can give their consent?"

Freya's ears perked as she, too, obviously wanted to know the answer.

He tilted his head from side to side. "Some. Those with a greater awareness."

"Like Freya?"

Freya blinked at me.

Gideon shook his head. "I would not bind Freya to me like that without your permission."

I met Freya's gaze, sensed that she wasn't totally against the idea, and then glanced back at him. "Not even if it would protect her?"

Gideon reached out and scratched her chin. Her immediate purring vibrated through me. "Freya is well protected at home and at Meowkins. Plus, she's fast, and she's smart. Don't worry, Daisy. Now that Sauron's made his intent perfectly clear, he won't be able to make a move without us knowing about it."

I shifted my stance. "But you said we were safe before."

He shrugged and nodded. "As I told your mother, I underestimated him. That won't happen again. Also, in my defense, I told you to not leave your shop, that I would drive you if you needed to go anywhere."

I gave him a look that owned my guilt. "I know. But..." I paused to release a heavy sigh. "It's been an awful morning, Gideon. Surreal. Nicole came in with bruises, saying she'd broken up with Cliff."

Black flickered in his eyes. "Where is this Cliff now? I'd like to have a word with him."

The fierceness in his voice left me with a shiver. "You can't. He's dead. Worse, they have Nicole at the station for questioning."

He tilted his head, his expression colored with disbelief. "They don't suspect her, do they?"

I shrugged. "I don't know. I hope not. But that's the reason I left Meowkins, to go with her to the station. After being there a while, I was advised to leave, so that's why I was out walking. I figured I'd be safe enough since it was daylight, people were around, and I didn't have far to go."

Muted anger emanated from him as he shook his head. "Sounds like we both underestimated him."

"I won't do it again either. The moment we're finished here, I'll try calling Corey again to see if he can tell me when Nicole will be released."

I glanced around us. "What do we need for this spell? Candles? Crystals? Fire?"

"No. Just a drop of my blood on the doorframe is enough. But if we combine power while I speak the incantation, it will make it that much more impenetrable."

I didn't hesitate to answer. "Yes. Of course. Anything to keep my mom safe."

He lifted a finger. "I'll be right back."

I watched as he returned to his car, studying the man that I loved. The way his long legs stretched as he strode, the ruffle of his hair when the breeze teased it, and I knew, despite some serious obstacles, he was the one for me.

When he returned, he carried a sheath the length of my hand with a black handle sticking out. I sensed formidable dark magic without trying and inhaled a deep breath. I lifted my gaze to him, caught him studying me.

"Are you sure you're okay with this?" he asked.

I swallowed and nodded. He wouldn't let me do anything that would harm me. "Yes, I trust you."

He placed his free hand over his heart. "Thank you."

Tiny sparks glittered as he unsheathed the black blade. I had no doubt the edge was razor sharp, unlike the athames witches used during rituals. The handle was ribbed, and the whole knife pulsed with masculine power. "Would you like to hold it?"

I exhaled and smiled. "Maybe another time. I sense it's power, and it feels very unfamiliar to me."

He nodded. "It's been passed down through my family. You're likely sensing those who came before me."

I looked at him hesitantly.

He tucked the sheath into his pocket, took my hand with his free one, and the energy of the knife flowed through him to me. It was pure Gideon. I exhaled and smiled. "That's better."

He approached the front door and then urged me forward. When I stood next to him, he met my gaze. "Place your ring finger in the hollow behind my ear."

I slid my fingers along his jawline until I located the spot. A rush of energy whipped through me, and I gasped.

He smiled. "Few humans are aware of this connectivity spot. We'd like to keep it that way."

I nodded my agreement.

"Hold your finger there while I complete the incantation. That's all that's required of you."

I gave a small shrug. "Seems simple enough."

"It may, but don't underestimate it any more than you would Sauron. If the power becomes too much, release me. Even a small contribution from you will help. Do you understand?"

"Yes," I said solemnly.

He sent me an encouraging smile. "Let's begin."

He focused on his hand. With the tip of the blade, he poked his ring finger and a tiny droplet of blood welled on the surface. Through our connection, I sensed the momentary flicker of pain.

Black licked at the edges of his irises, giving me chills. I knew it was only a visual of his power, but it still unnerved me. He touched the tiny dot of red to an inconspicuous spot between two bricks.

I glanced upward at the house, grateful that my mom couldn't see this spot from any of her windows.

Gideon shifted, drawing my attention. "You may close your eyes if that will help you focus."

I released a small chuckle knowing that he'd likely guessed at my thoughts. "Okay."

I licked my bottom lip and closed my eyes. Freya rubbed against my legs, and I sensed her trying to add her power to mine.

With no other sensory interfering, the bond between us seemed to strengthen. I couldn't understand the words he whispered, but the power of them washed through me like wild ocean waves, giving and taking as it did.

The only problem was that the spell began to feel as if it was taking increasingly more. I tried to focus on my mom, on adding my power to the spell to keep her safe, but my legs reminded me that they'd already had one good workout that day.

I wondered if I should release him, but then I felt like I could go a little longer, knowing every bit would help. When he finished, something akin to a sonic wave rolled through me, and my legs decided they'd had enough.

I drew my hand away from his neck and grasped for his arm as I went down. He caught me immediately, tried to help me stand, but my legs refused to hold my weight.

Fear licked at my thoughts. "What's happening?"

Gideon cursed under his breath, but his response was cut off by the sound of locks turning. It was bad enough that I couldn't stand, but I knew all hell would break loose if my mother knew that Gideon had taken so much energy from me. Or even the fact that he could take a little.

I gripped the back of his neck and jerked him toward me. "Kiss me."

Our lips met just as the door opened. "What on the Goddess's green earth...*oh*. Take that somewhere else."

Before I could react, my mom promptly shut the door.

Relief mingled with apprehension over my current state. I lifted my gaze to Gideon and found concern still hovering there. "Can you stand?" he whispered.

I tried again and failed. When I shook my head, the worry in his voice darkened with anger. "I told you to release me if it became too much."

Irritated frustration rolled through me. "Obviously, I didn't know what too much was."

He shook his head in disappointment.

"Can we talk about this in the car?" I asked in a harsh whisper. "I don't want to be here if my mom opens the door again. Can you just help me walk?"

He scoffed. "You can't even stand."

That fact did worry me a little. Maybe more than a little. Though I knew I wasn't paralyzed. It was more that I was overwhelmingly weak. "Just give me a minute. I can feel my strength coming back."

Before I could come up with a solution, he scooped me up and headed down the walkway toward his car.

"Wait. What if my mother or Mona looks out the window?"

"You can't have it both ways, Daisy. Either we sit here until you're better, which might be a while, or I carry you and let them think I'm carting you off to a dark cave somewhere to ravish your soul."

"Not funny."

He pinned me with a look that said he agreed, and I swallowed my smart-mouthed retort.

Getting me into his car wasn't easy, but I honestly did feel a little stronger. At least I thought I did. I brought my knees together to prove that everything still worked.

Freya jumped onto my lap and began sniffing me furiously. I drew my brows in worry. "This isn't permanent, right?"

He flashed me a quick look before starting his engine, anger pulsating from his expression. "I'd like to give you a dose of fear and tell you that it is. Then maybe you'll listen to me next time, but no. You'll need some time to recover, but that's all."

"That's good."

I thought he'd pull out onto the street, but instead, he rounded on me. "*It's not good, Daisy. I never would have trusted you with my magic if I'd known you couldn't handle yours.*"

I blinked and dropped my jaw. It took a moment for my irritation to build and give me back my voice. "What do you mean? I can handle my magic just fine."

He lifted a hand to stop me. I clenched my jaw, wanting to rant at him, but I held my tongue for the moment.

He shifted his Mercedes into gear and took off toward home at an incredible speed. We both remained silent on the drive, and as the miles passed, I felt his anger dissipating. By the time we reached home, he seemed much calmer.

I hadn't managed to release my irritation so easily. If I could have, I would have headed straight into the house without him. Instead, I simmered as he exited the car and strode to my side.

Worse, I'd begun to shiver. I didn't know if it was from the realization of what had happened to me, the overuse of my magic, or from participating in a blood spell.

Because that's exactly what Gideon had used.

He opened my door, and Freya jumped from my lap. I met his gaze, trying to keep my emotions in check. I shifted on the seat to prove that I wasn't as weak as he thought I was, but when I tried to stand, I couldn't. He scooped me from the car. As he carried me toward the cottage, I heard the door slam shut behind us.

Inside, he sat me on the couch, wrapped a soft throw about my shoulders and placed a small quilt across my lap. "You're shivering."

I frowned. "I know."

He shook his head and then closed his eyes for a moment. When he looked at me again, worry had crept back into his expression. "I'm sorry I yelled at you. This was my fault. I should have known."

My frown deepened. "If you're trying to make me feel better, you aren't."

He nodded slowly. "Tell me what I can do to help you."

"First, you can stop acting like I'm a child who can't take care of myself."

He lifted his brows to challenge my claim and then glanced toward my legs.

I folded my arms in front of me. "Fine. I understand that I took on too much. This was the first time I've...participated in that kind of magic. I had no way of knowing my limitations."

He snorted and shook his head. "But *I* should have known."

His expression turned to one of serious contemplation. "The problem is that when I touch you, I feel your power so strongly. I guess I hadn't realized that you were a novice when it came to using it."

My anger reengaged full force. "I'm not a novice. I've been a witch for forty years. I know what I'm doing."

He arched his brow. "Do you?"

I licked my bottom lip that wouldn't stop quivering and swallowed. I glanced about the room and then focused on Freya who sat on the floor near my feet, regarding me with a questioning look. I'd obviously gotten in way over my head that night, but how was I to know what might have happened?

I dropped my gaze to my lap. "I don't want to talk about it anymore. I'd just like to go to bed."

Gideon released a heavy sigh. "You need something to warm your insides. It will help you recover faster. I'll make tea and some soup."

My teeth chattered too much to argue.

As he walked away, a fire roared to life in the fireplace, even though we were in the heat of summer.

EIGHT

I woke the next morning, a snuggled up, sweating mess and flung the bed covers from me. Freya must have been in the line of fire because she meowed her complaint and dashed from the bed. If I didn't know better, I would have thought I was in the throes of a vicious hot flash.

When I found only Old Grey and not Gideon asleep on his side of the bed, I opened my senses and realized Gideon had already left the cottage. I wondered if he'd bothered to go to bed the previous night. I'd fallen asleep so fast that I had no clue.

I sat up and stretched, every muscle aching like I'd worked out at the Expanding Universe for a whole day straight. I scooted to the edge of the bed and cautiously tested my weight. When my legs held, I exhaled my relief. Thank the Goddess for her healing miracles.

Just when I thought everything would be okay, I checked the messages on my phone and found at least ten from Aeri along with many missed calls. Scrolling through, I found that they went from curious, to edgy, to downright angry that I hadn't contacted her. I glanced at the clock and realized my coffee shop would have been open for an hour already.

I groaned, knowing I had a lot of explaining to do. I quickly sent a message to Aeri apologizing and promising to tell her everything once I was at the café. I'd barely made it down the hall when my phone rang.

One glance at the screen told me it was Aeri, and I didn't need anyone or anything to tell me it wouldn't be a pleasant, chatty conversation. I braced myself and tapped the answer button.

"Good Goddess, lady. Where have you been?"

I winced. It took a lot to ruffle Aeri, and I sensed I'd gone far past that point. "I'm so sorry. I should have—"

"Do you even care about Nicole? Or me? I fretted for hours until Nicole called me to pick her up from the police station. Did you forget that our friend was hauled down there yesterday on suspicion of murder?"

Suddenly, the strength I'd regained overnight seemed to fizzle. "Of course, I didn't forget." Though if I was honest, Nicole hadn't been first on my mind that morning, and I regretted that immensely. "I had a really bad day—"

"Worse than Nicole?"

Some of my fire returned. "Look, I'm sorrier than you could imagine that I wasn't there for her, okay? Since the moment Corey took her away, everything spiraled out of control."

"Yeah, I know. You promised to tell me everything. But here it is almost a day later, and I'm barely hearing from you."

"I did blood magic."

I hadn't meant to blurt it out like that, but it seemed the only way to get her to give me a chance to speak. And it did exactly that. If I didn't know better, I would think she'd hung up.

"You did what?"

I sighed. "I would really like to tell you this in person."

"Tell me now."

I supposed I didn't have much of a choice. "Yesterday after Sauron chased me down, Gideon insisted on protecting my mom's house. He'd said that if I added my power to his, the spell or incantation would be that much stronger. I can't let my mom be hurt by anything that I'm tangled up in, so I agreed. When he brought out his knife to draw blood—"

"You didn't give your blood, *did you?*"

"No. Of course not. For some stupid reason, I didn't even realize we were doing blood magic until later. But it wasn't dark magic. It was for good. To protect my mom."

"But something happened."

Her comment wasn't even a question.

"Yeah. I...before we combined powers, Gideon warned me not to give too much. But I realized later that I didn't know what that meant, and unfortunately, I overextended myself to the point that my legs gave out. And then I started shivering."

Aeri gasped. "But you should have known when you'd reached your limits."

I clenched my jaw in frustration. "Obviously, I didn't, or I would've stopped."

I was done explaining my actions. "Look. It was unfortunate, but I'm okay. I slept like the dead, and I'm doing better. I'm sorry I was so out of it that I didn't check on Nicole. Where is she? How is she?"

Aeri sighed. "She's not good. I picked her up yesterday evening after they released her, and she spent the night at my house. She's not coming in to work today, obviously. She wants to get some things from their house, but she wants to talk to you first."

I felt like the worst friend ever. "Maybe I should just close the shop today. We're all a mess, and Nicole needs us."

"Lucky for you, I've got your back. Sailor's here again, and she brought Alisha with her. Alisha has some cashiering experience, so I have her on the counter while I handle the orders. Plus, it's a slow day."

Gratitude for my friend tugged on my heart. "I don't deserve you."

"Of course, you do. But you need to get your act together. Nicole needs us. I know you have that demon stuff going on, but you need to let Gideon handle it and stop messing with things that are over your head."

I wanted to argue with her, but I couldn't when she was currently saving my butt. "Thank you."

Aeri hesitated for a long moment, making me fear what else she had to say. "I'm going to tell you now because you'll sense it as soon as you come into the shop. I've used magic a few times here this morning. You didn't show, and I had people waiting at the door first thing. I did what I had to do."

I frowned. "So?"

"So?" She sounded shocked. "You're the one who's against using our powers here."

Her words surprised me. "I never said you couldn't."

She scoffed. "Pretty much. You made it clear that you preferred not to on a day-to-day basis."

I shook my head, confused. "No. I...I just...I'm not against magic."

She snorted. "Could have fooled me. Up until recently, you haven't wanted much of it in your life."

"That's not true. I just preferred to practice as a solitary witch. I didn't use it every day because it didn't seem necessary."

Several moments passed before Aeri spoke again. "Oh, lady. We have a lot to talk about. But you need to help Nicole first. I've got work covered. You take care of our girl."

I promised I would and then ended the call.

For a moment, the room seemed to spin, and I closed my eyes. I needed to get my feet back under me figuratively and literally. There was no time to falter now.

I made a quick call to Nicole, who was much more pleasant on the phone, and she agreed to let me explain once I picked her up from Aeri's house.

I dressed and ate a quick breakfast before I picked up my purse and headed for the front door.

Freya raced forward from out of nowhere and blocked my path. *No.*

I tilted my head at her. "I need to help Nicole."

You can't leave alone.

Bless the Great Goddess. I didn't know how I could have, but I'd completely forgotten that it wasn't safe for me to be out alone. Seriously, that blood spell must have hit me harder than I'd realized.

I scooped up my cat and hugged her against me. "Yes, you're right. I'm sorry. My head isn't working properly this morning. I'll call Gideon."

He answered on the first ring. "Are you okay?"

I wasn't sure if he meant mentally or physically, but I answered in the affirmative. "I'm supposed to help Nicole move her things today. Could you drive me?"

"I left my car for you. You'll be safe there. But it's risky for you to be at Nicole's. What time were you planning to go?"

I grimaced. "Uh, now?"

"Okay. I'll make sure we're close by while you're there. Take Freya. If you feel even a prick of danger, go straight to my car."

I paused while I replayed his last statement. "You're going to let me go out alone?"

"You'll have Freya. She can sense Sauron."

I shook my head to clear it. "And you know this how?"

"She told me."

I glanced at my familiar and lifted my brows. "I wish she'd tell me some of this. She's my familiar after all."

He gave a small chuckle. "I think she tried yesterday morning. She mentioned something about crystals."

I thought back to her playing with my hematite on the kitchen floor. She didn't seem like she'd been trying very hard to communicate with me then, but hematite was known for its protective properties. "Maybe she did. I'll be sure to take her and check in with you, okay?"

He exhaled. "Daisy?"

"Yes?"

"I love you. Please be safe."

His heartfelt sentiment warmed me. "I'll be as careful as I can, and I love you, too."

NINE

D riving down the lushly forested mountain with Freya in the passenger seat of Gideon's sleek, black Mercedes did lift my mood. At least as much as it could knowing a demon bent on revenge was after me and one of my best friends was a murder suspect. But the way the car smoothly took the curves was a delight to my senses.

When I pulled into Aeri's driveway, it seemed strange to see Nicole emerge instead. She still wore the same Meowkins t-shirt that she'd had on the previous day, reminding me that she'd had a hellish time of it since we'd last seen each other. I wanted to get out of the car and hug her but decided that the more I played it safe, the better off for everyone.

Freya moved to the center console when Nicole opened the car door and climbed in. My friend shut the door, and the moment she turned to me, the tears started. Freya immediately jumped onto her lap.

My heart broke for her. "Oh, Nicole."

I reached across the console and pulled her into my embrace. "I'm so sorry I wasn't reachable last night. I'll explain later, but know that I feel terrible for letting you down."

She wiped her eyes and sniffed. "You didn't, Daisy. You helped me with Corey and helped me find a place to stay. Aeri told me some of what happened after my arrest, and she was able to pick me up last night. Don't worry about it."

I released her. "I worry about *you*. I won't ask if you're okay, because obviously you're not. Is there anything I can do for you?"

She gave a small shrug. "Only what you're already doing. Your mom called a while ago to ask when I'd arrive. Thanks for setting that up for me."

I nodded. "You know she loves you. To be fair, she'd probably rather see you than me, anyway."

Nicole shook her head, and I snorted. "No, really. You'll see once we get to her house."

She gave me a doubtful look. "Anyway, I told her it wouldn't take us long at my old place. I just want to get a few things for now and get settled. I don't want to be in there where he died for very long."

I backed the car onto the street. "I can understand that."

Nicole fidgeted as we made our way toward the house that she and Cliff had rented when they'd moved in together.

"Hang in there. We'll be in and out as fast as possible. If we use our magic, it will go even faster."

She drew her brows in question. "You're okay with that?"

I couldn't believe that I'd given off the impression that I didn't like the gift the Goddess had given me. "Why wouldn't I be okay with it? My mom and I used magic to pack my house when I had to move."

She shrugged. "You've always seemed biased against it for the most part, preferring to do things the human way."

I denied it with a shake of my head. "That wasn't because I have an aversion to the craft. At Meowkins, I didn't want to chase away customers who were uneducated about witchcraft. Other times, it seemed to be a waste of energy that I wanted to conserve for other things."

She seemed confused. "But the more you use it, the stronger you get and the less energy it requires."

I'd learned that lesson the hard way. "No one ever told me that," I said quietly, embarrassed to be my age and still not know everything about the power in my blood.

Nicole shifted in her seat to face me, still looking teary-eyed. "I can't believe your mom didn't. Why wouldn't she?"

I shook my head slowly. "I don't know. Either way, let's stop talking about me. What you're going through is more important."

"I'd rather talk about you than me. It's a good distraction."

I sent her a consoling smile. "We'll get through this together."

As we neared her former home, Nicole released a defeated sigh. "Corey said he'd meet us at the house. We need a police escort to go inside since it's still a crime scene. They want to know what I'm taking with me."

I kept my reaction of disgust to myself and instead spoke in a calm voice. "That doesn't mean that they think you're guilty. I'm sure it's just protocol."

She turned to look out the window. "It doesn't feel routine to me. It's personal."

I wished I knew what I could say to bring her peace. "I'm sure it's only until they clear you. What if you accidentally took something that was important to the case, you know? They're just being conscientious."

She gave me a doubtful look and then focused out the windshield as we pulled up in front of the small gray duplex with shrubbery planted along the foundation. Two police cruisers were also there, and I spotted Corey near the porch waiting for us.

He lifted a hand in greeting as I killed the engine, and I did the same. After the incident the previous day when we'd found ourselves on opposite sides, I felt better knowing that he still wanted a friendly relationship.

I turned to Nicole. "Try not to think too much while we're here. Just focus on what you need and push everything else to the background. You can work through your grief and other things at another time when you're feeling safe, okay?"

She exhaled a shaky breath and snuggled Freya tighter against her.

I'd barely stepped out of the driver's seat when a slick silver car turned onto the street behind me and cruised slowly toward us with the sun glinting off its polished paint. We had our share of nice cars in town, but not in this neighborhood. My internal alarms kicked in.

"Nicole," I warned over the roof of Gideon's car. "Wait a minute. Show me Freya. She's not acting alarmed, is she?"

Nicole lifted the gray bundle of fur in her arms up next to her face so that I could see her. "She seems fine to me."

"Everything okay?" Corey called out as he started walking toward us.

I lifted a hand to let him know we were fine and focused on my familiar just to be sure. "Anything amiss, Freya?"

She meowed her everyday meow and then suddenly turned her head toward the oncoming car. Her quick actions startled me, and I was about to announce that we should all get back inside, but her eyes brightened, and she started to purr.

Gideon.

Her thoughts came to me loud and clear. I glanced at the car once more, and now that it was closer, I could see Gideon sitting in the passenger seat.

A man with dark sunglasses and a stark white shirt sat behind the wheel of the BMW sedan. If I didn't know better, I'd think the two men were mafia. The driver, who I could only assume was Gideon's boss, pulled up next to the Mercedes, and Gideon stepped from the car. He searched my face as though ensuring I was okay. "Hello, my lovely. We were nearby, and I wanted to check in with you."

Before I could reply, he turned his head and focused on something beyond me. The love in his beautiful blue eyes flipped to one of wariness, and I knew he'd noticed Corey.

I reached out and touched Gideon's cheek, drawing his gaze back to me. "Everything's fine."

Irritation flickered in his eyes. "Does he have to be here?"

I nodded. "A police chaperone is the only way they'll let Nicole in the house, and I'd rather have Corey than anyone else. He's a friend to her, too."

Gideon lifted his chin in what could barely be considered agreement. He briefly kissed me on the cheek before he strode to the opposite side of the car. He opened his arms to Nicole, and she leaned into him. My heart broke all over again when I heard her sobs.

He held her and stroked her hair, pausing to give Freya a few pets since she was squished between them. "It's going to be okay, my dear. We're here for you. I'll do whatever I can to help, and you know Daisy will be relentless until the person who's responsible is behind bars."

Nicole lifted her gaze and stepped back. "Thank you, Gideon. I appreciate that so much."

He nodded and petted Freya again. "This little one will help you, too. You're not alone."

Nicole gave him a watery smile that tugged at my heart. That was until I felt a powerful presence come up behind me. I turned and inhaled sharply when I came face-to-face with Gideon's boss.

He stood several inches taller than me, and I felt the weight of his shadow. His raven black hair and dark goatee made him appear that much more ominous. The scar running above his left eyebrow didn't help, either. I wished I could see behind the sunglasses and into his eyes.

The man cleared his throat, and Gideon turned to him.

"This is the one?" he said without taking his gaze off me.

I couldn't look away to see what expression Gideon had on his face, but I sensed his happiness. "That she is. Daisy, I'd like you to meet my boss, Antonio Calabrese. Antonio, this is Daisy Summers, my love."

The fact that he'd had no qualms introducing me that way caught me off guard. A blush heated my cheeks, and I held out a hand, hoping to get a sense of the intimidating demon through physical contact. "Very nice to meet you, Mr. Calabrese."

He wrapped strong, warm fingers around mine and held them there. "Please," he said in a voice that purred with charisma. "Call me Antonio."

I nodded as engaging energy, not as pure as Gideon's, passed through his hand to me. "Very nice to meet you, Antonio."

He released my hand. "It's my pleasure to meet the one Gideon talks about so often."

Interactions with strangers weren't my strong suit, and with so much power emanating from him, I admit it left me dizzy. "Thank you. Uh, this is my friend, Nicole. She's going through a rough time right now."

Antonio dipped his head. "My condolences on your loss, Ms. Santoro."

She nodded her thanks and then focused on Freya.

I shouldn't have been surprised that Antonio knew what had happened or that he knew Nicole's last name, but I was. Gideon must have mentioned her.

I looked from him, noticed Corey standing midway on the lawn with his feet spread, his arms folded, and an unfriendly look on his face, and then I turned to Gideon. "We should get going. I'd like to get Nicole to my mom's as soon as possible."

He strode toward me and held my shoulders as he gave me a quick kiss. "We'll be nearby if you need us."

"Thanks, Gideon."

He gave Corey one more glance before he released me. I waved goodbye to Antonio, and they entered the sparkling silver BMW. The engine rumbled with power when Antonio started it, and they cruised away.

TEN

I blew out a breath to release the awkwardness of the interaction with Gideon's boss while Corey hovered not far away, and I headed toward Nicole. When I reached her, I slipped my hand around her elbow. "Let's get this done."

We walked together with her carrying Freya to where Corey waited in the middle of the lawn. I met his gaze and smiled to set my intention for a pleasant interaction. "Good morning."

He adjusted the ball cap covering his blond hair and jutted his chin toward the retreating red car. "Who was that with your boyfriend?"

I withheld a sigh of frustration and kept my smile in place. "His boss. He's in town for a few days."

He arched his brow. "Boss, huh? He looks like a mob boss. What line of work?"

Nicole squared her jaw in a show of solidarity. "We're here to collect my things, not be interrogated again."

I gave Corey a small shrug. "She's right. That conversation can wait for another day."

Or never.

He swept his hand toward the front door. "After you, ladies."

I gave Nicole's elbow a squeeze, and we moved forward. At the door, she turned the knob and pushed it open.

Instead of stepping forward, she faced me. "I don't know if I can do this."

I nodded encouragingly. "Just focus on what you need right now. When it's time to clear everything out, Aeri and I will come with you or do it for you, okay? Let's just get what you need to take to my mom's."

She released a weighted breath and entered the house. Overwhelming residual anger and fear hit me the moment we walked inside. Nicole inhaled sharply, and she stumbled.

"Focus," I whispered and directed her toward their bedroom, opposite of the kitchen where the murder had occurred.

Corey stood inside the bedroom door while Nicole and I pulled clothing from drawers and her side of the closet. She didn't speak, and I could tell that she was barely keeping herself composed, which made me work faster.

When that was finished, I glanced at Corey who nodded his consent, and we zipped her two suitcases closed. Nicole sat on the edge of the bed, dropped her face into her hand, and quietly cried.

I placed a hand on her shoulder to comfort her. "I'm sure you'll want things from the bathroom."

She nodded but didn't move. I glanced at Corey who gave me a sad smile and shook his head as if he didn't know what to do.

I patted her back. "Let me get them for you, okay? You can wait in the car with Freya."

At the sound of her name, Freya jumped on the bed next to Nicole and rubbed against her side. Without looking up, Nicole reached for my kitty and lifted her into her arms. She stood and walked woodenly toward the door.

I was going to ask if she wanted anything specific but decided to let her go instead. I'd just take everything that looked like it belonged to her.

Corey stood, grabbed the handles of the two suitcases, and followed behind Nicole. "Be right back."

I blew out a breath full of stress. It was hard to watch one of my best friends suffer, and I could only imagine how much worse it was for her.

The only thing I could find to carry her toiletries was a small garbage bag beneath the sink. I grabbed her shampoo, hair brush, and face wash along with various other things and placed them in a group on the vanity. I opted out of taking a toothbrush for fear that I might not get the right one.

I had everything I thought was hers sitting out by the time Corey returned. I glanced up at him. "Is she okay?"

He shrugged. "Not especially. She's in the front seat hugging Freya as tightly as she can."

Gratitude for my familiar filled me. "Freya will take good care of her."

Then I pointed to everything on the counter. "This is what I plan to take, okay?"

He briefly glanced at the collection and then focused on me. "I trust you, Daisy."

I lifted my brow. "But you don't trust Nicole?"

Regret dimmed his features. "It's not that I don't trust her. It's that I can't right now."

I dropped my shoulders and exhaled. "I know. I'm sorry. I'm just really frustrated by everything. Cliff never loved her like she deserved, and now he's made her life even more miserable."

Corey tilted his head and lifted a corner of his mouth. "You mean the person who killed him made her life harder."

I lifted my hands in defeat. "They both have. If you can tell me that you've found another suspect besides Nicole, that would go a long way."

He pinned me with a direct look. "No one, so far. Nicole couldn't name anyone who might want to harm Cliff. The people he worked with didn't know much about him outside of work. Some of them didn't even know he lived with Nicole. Obviously, we'll dig deeper, look at phone records and bank accounts, but in addition to that, I wanted to ask for your help."

I shifted my gaze to the toiletries and began placing them in the bag. "You know that it's highly unlikely that I'd tell you anything that I might learn in regards to Nicole."

He stepped farther into the bathroom. "That makes it sound like you believe she might have something to hide."

I flashed an irritated look at him. "Of course, I don't. She's one of the gentlest souls I know."

He gave me a knowing nod. "I'm not asking you to spy on her, Daisy. We had a hard time getting much information out of her during the interview yesterday. She was too upset."

"Obviously."

He sent me a look that questioned my attitude, and regret slid in. "Sorry. Again. It's just the investigation is making things so much harder on her, and you're the one behind that."

"That's fair. But by helping me, you'll be helping her, too. All I need is for you to question her a little, see if you can get her to recall any incidents where Cliff might have angered someone. If she's not feeling threatened and can take her time, she might remember someone or something."

I finished packing and faced him. "Of course, I will. Honestly, you know I would have done that anyway."

He smiled. "No doubt. But I'm making an official request regardless."

I stared at him for a long moment, sensed the interest burning in him, and was grateful that he didn't act on it. Much. "I'll do what I can."

He gave me a quick nod. "Thank you for that. I'll let you get back to Nicole. Getting her settled is a good first step to healing."

He was a wise man. I'd give him that. "Thanks. Talk soon."

With that, I gathered the edges of the bag holding Nicole's things and strode from the bathroom to the front door and out into the sunny day that belied everything I felt inside. I glanced around, looking for Sauron and then used my senses to search as well. Then I hurried toward the beautiful black Mercedes.

By the time I was in the driver's seat, Nicole had stopped crying. She stroked Freya's soft gray fur, and my cat's purr echoed through the quiet car.

Nicole met my gaze, her eyes bloodshot and her eyelids swollen. "Why don't I have a familiar?"

I started the engine and shrugged. "I don't know. Why don't you?"

"I guess I've never searched for one, and if there's one meant for me somewhere out there, it hasn't found its way to me, either. When I first started working for you, I'd hoped I might encounter mine at the Parlor, but it seems everyone else gets one but me."

I reached over and squeezed her hand. "Fatalistic thinking isn't going to make you feel any better. You, out of everyone that I know, deserves a familiar. Don't give up hope just yet."

Though she didn't meet my gaze, she kissed Freya's head and nodded.

I turned the car around and headed toward my mother's.

After several minutes of silence, I decided it was as good a time as any to question Nicole. Although I knew she was hurting, the sooner we cleared her name, the better.

I glanced across the car toward her. "Just so you know, I don't think Corey believes that you did it."

She cautiously lifted her gaze to me. "How can you be sure?"

"He asked me to help him. Right now, you're the only suspect, but he's searching for others. He said that you didn't give him any helpful information."

"That's because I don't have any. Trust me, if I could focus the blame somewhere else, I would."

A car turned onto the road behind me, and I glanced repeatedly in the rearview mirror. But then it turned again, and I was fairly certain it belonged to Wanda who worked at a clothing boutique on Main Street. "Corey thought maybe if we put our heads together and spent some time talking, that it might jog your memory. Maybe there was a minor incident. Or maybe Cliff casually mentioned someone in conversation, but you were unable to recall yesterday because you were in shock."

Nicole remained quiet for several moments and then shook her head. "I can't think of anyone. Honestly, Cliff was one of the most boring guys. All he cared about was beer and ballgames."

"What about his friends? I can't recall you ever mentioning any."

She shook her head. "That's because he didn't really have them. They took too much effort."

I shot her a pitiful glance. Not that I had tons of friends, either, but the ones I did have were precious to me.

She huffed. "Look, I know he sounds like a loser. Honestly, he was. But he's my loser." Her voice broke. "At least, he was."

I needed to remember that up until the previous day, she and Cliff had been a couple. And Nicole wouldn't have remained with him if she didn't love him at least a little and if she didn't have hope that they'd make things work. "I know. Even though he'd hurt you and you'd broken up, you still cared for the guy."

She blinked back tears and nodded. "I did."

I'd planned to give her a few moments to recover before I asked my next question, but she jumped right back in. "He did have one friend. A guy named Roger Evans. He only mentioned him a few times, and I never met him, so I don't think they saw much of each other."

I mentally made a note of his name. "Maybe he might know of someone who would want to hurt Cliff."

She shook her head. "I doubt it. I don't think Cliff had any enemies. Well, except maybe his crazy sister. But she lives somewhere out of state, and they haven't spoken in years."

I turned onto the street where my mother lived and parked in front of the house. Instead of immediately going inside, I slid my gaze to Nicole. "Still, she probably ought to be notified, don't you think? Did he have other family?"

"I don't think so. He told me once when he was drunk that his parents were dead. I wouldn't know how to contact his sister though. The only thing I know is that he'd called her Crazy Carly."

I nodded in approval. "Maybe someone at the police department can track her down. Crazy Carly. I'm guessing her last name would have been the same as his at some point in her life."

The look she gave me said that she wasn't convinced. "His mom wasn't married when she had Cliff, but he did mention a step-dad. His sister might have that guy's last name."

I paused to think. "Did Cliff ever mention his mom's first name?"

She shook her head. "No. But I'm sure it's on his birth certificate if they can locate that information."

I sent her a smile full of love and understanding. "I know you don't think it's much, but the things you've told me might lead somewhere. It's better to give the police the smallest details than nothing at all."

She sighed. "Yeah. I'm sure you're right. Can we go inside now? This day has already been too long, and I want it to be done."

"Of course."

I glanced about and then kept an eye on Freya, looking for any sign of disturbance, as Nicole and I carried her suitcases and bag of toiletries to my mom's front door. I tested the door knob, found it locked, and was relieved. At least she'd taken my warnings seriously.

I set down the suitcase and bag to search my purse for the house key.

"There's something here, isn't there?" Nicole asked softly. "A dark spell."

I stopped searching and turned to her. "There is. It's a protection spell."

"It's powerful. Blood magic."

I hadn't realized Nicole was so intuitive, but I supposed we hadn't talked much witchcraft until recently. "Yes. Gideon claimed her house so that no other demon could enter uninvited. You'll be protected while you're staying here, too."

She nodded. "Aeri said that Sauron had bothered you."

Bothered might have been a little tame for what had happened, but Aeri had probably kept information to a minimum because the last thing Nicole needed was more worry. "He's not a good person, Nicole."

"Did Gideon claim you, too? To protect you?"

Her question caught me off guard. "No. That's a more serious issue from what I understand. But he did protect Meowkins, the cottage, and his car."

She sighed. "I wish Cliff could have been more like Gideon. I wish he could have loved me that way."

I didn't want to tell her that if that was the case, she'd be buried in grief right now instead of just suffering. Instead, I agreed with a nod and went back to fishing for my keys.

Before I found them, my mom opened the door and urged us to come inside. Nicole went first, and my mom enveloped her in a motherly hug. Before I stepped over the threshold, I shot a quick glance to where Gideon had left a drop of his blood, and the sight of it left me with a shiver.

ELEVEN

Once I was inside, my mom released Nicole and closed the door behind us. Freya jumped from Nicole's arms and headed into the kitchen where my mom would likely have treats waiting for her. Freya was the closest thing she'd have to a grandchild, and she loved spoiling her.

My mom glanced at the suitcases we held. "I have Daisy's old room ready for you Nicole. Let's get you unpacked and settled in."

Nicole blinked back emotion. "If it's okay with you guys, I'd like to be alone for a while. I don't have much, and I can unpack later. I just want to shower and sleep."

"Of course," my mom said. "But only if you'll let me bring you some iced tea and a muffin. Freshly-baked."

Nicole gave her a grateful smile. "Thanks."

I jutted my head toward my old bedroom. "Come on. I'll carry these in for you."

I helped Nicole settle, brought the tray of two muffins, sliced cheddar cheese, and grapes along with the iced tea from my mom, and then let her be. I could see in her eyes that she was weary beyond measure.

Then I searched for my mom and found her in her favorite chair in the sitting room. She glanced from her view of the towering picturesque mountains to me and gave me a sad smile. "She'll be okay."

I nodded. "I know. It's just rough watching her go through this and not being able to do much to help."

My mom shook her head in distaste. "I can't believe Corey took her in for questioning. He should have known better."

"Same. But I know he's only doing his job. One way or the other, he had to question her. She knew more about Cliff than any of us. It's just awful the way everything went down."

My mom pointed to the couch, and I noticed that she had a pitcher of iced tea and two glasses sitting on a tray on the coffee table. "Come and sit."

I really wasn't up for another heated discussion about Gideon, or worse, another intervention, but I supposed we needed to talk. I sat on the couch near her and watched as she poured tea into both glasses. "This seems perfect today. Thank you."

She smiled, deepening the lines next to her eyes. "I figured you could use something refreshing. Have a muffin, too. They're really good, if I do say so myself."

I knew they would be. I accepted the glass and added extra sugar. "Thanks."

I sipped the iced tea, letting the cool liquid soothe my stress. Then I plated a muffin and sat back on the couch. I pinched off a piece and placed it in my mouth. When the flavors hit my tongue, I groaned in appreciation. "It's been a busy morning, and I didn't have time for much breakfast."

My mother nodded. "A busy yesterday followed by a busy today."

I knew the topic was inevitable, but I didn't want to ruin the peace of the moment. "Yeah. It's all a little surreal. First learning of Nicole's bruises and the break up, then that Cliff was killed, followed by..."

"That demon," my mother finished for me.

I nodded.

She heaved a weighted sigh. "I'll admit that Gideon did a good job with the protection spell outside, though I loathe having demon blood on my doorstep."

I widened my eyes. "You know about the blood?"

She snorted. "Did you think I would miss it?"

I'd thought that she might, but I didn't tell her so. "He wanted you to have the strongest protection. I know you don't like him, but he was worried about you."

She took a drink of iced tea and then regarded me with an arched brow. "If he cared so much, he wouldn't put my daughter in danger."

I held up a hand and shook my head. "I don't want to rehash the same conversation."

She cleared her throat. "I know that you helped with the spell, too."

I stared at her.

Her gaze seemed to pierce my soul. "I can sense even now what it cost you. Don't think I don't appreciate it."

I nodded in response. "You're welcome."

She held my gaze for a long moment. "You should have known better though, Daisy. As inexperienced as you are, it could have hurt you."

I snorted in disagreement. "I'm a fully grown witch, Mum. And I had Gideon there. Most of the magic was his."

She remained silent, irritating me further. "What? Just say it."

A long sigh filled the quiet. "You're a fully grown *woman*, but you're dealing with powerful magical beings here. Ones that you have no business being around."

Being around? I wasn't a silly groupie. Gideon and I loved each other. I scrunched my features. "I'm a magical being, too."

She hesitated again, and the bud of annoyance inside me bloomed.

"Look, Daisy. You might have witch blood, and apparently, it's stronger than I realized. But you've never honed your craft. You've left it sitting by the wayside for the most part, which was fully your choice, and I respected that. But thinking that your powers are what they could have been is like entering a neglected and overgrown garden and expecting to find prized tomatoes."

What they could have been? She made it sound like I was over the hill with no way back to the top. "I've practiced my craft," I said in defense. "And I would have been stronger if you'd told me that the more often that I used my magic, the less energy spells would ultimately require."

A sarcastic tone accompanied her chuckle. "You know, I often wondered if this day would come. I'd hoped for it, hoped you would someday decide to fully accept your gift. But I knew you wouldn't be happy about the time you'd wasted when you did."

I folded my arms, unhappy with everything that had happened the past couple of days. "So, I'm just a lost cause. Is that it? Should I break up with Gideon, resign from the coven's council, and go back to only running Meowkins and not having much of anything else in my life?"

She calmly took a sip of iced tea while she studied me over the rim of her glass. "You're angry."

I gasped. "Yes, Mum. I'm angry. My best friend has been accused of murder, you hate the man that I love, and everyone, including you, seems to think my magic is inconsequential."

"You're putting words in my mouth. I did not say that."

I snorted. "You might as well have."

She stared at me for a long moment and then nodded. "You have a fire in you, Daisy, that I haven't seen before. Your aura radiates it, too."

I couldn't tell if she meant that as a compliment or not. "What do you mean?"

"Jocelyn seems to think you have great potential. Usually, that's discovered long before a witch turns forty. It seems you might be a late bloomer."

I supposed that was better than never blooming. "Does she?"

My mother nodded and then shifted a quick sideways glance at her magical chest.

"Why did you just look there?"

She widened her eyes with innocence. "Where?"

"Hello, Mum. I just saw you look at your special chest. Why?"

She gazed into her glass a moment before she focused on me again. "Jocelyn believes I should pass the family grimoire along to you, but I'm not sure you're ready."

A spark of excitement lit inside me and inflamed my whole body when I inhaled a deep breath. "If you don't think I'm ready now, then you probably never will. Not to mention, if I must wait until you've passed into the next life, I'll be left all alone with the grimoire and no one to guide me. I might go crazy and start doing blood spells for the fun of it."

She frowned at me. "Not funny."

I might have gone over the top, but I'd had enough of people telling me my magic was basically worthless. "No, it's not funny. I'm sitting here before you, more ready than I've ever been to learn. There's a demon who'd like to hurt me, and you're willing to leave me at his mercy without a chance to become stronger."

She dropped her face into her hand for a moment and sighed. "Ah, Daisy. Sometimes, I wish we could go back to when you were five. Life was much simpler then."

"I haven't been five for a long time, Mum."

She nodded and stood. My pulse jumped when she began walking toward her chest. I couldn't believe I might have successfully convinced her.

She whispered something, and the lid of the ornate, old chest lifted. With her back to me, she bent, reached inside, and then straightened. When she turned, she clutched a thick, brown leather-bound volume in her hands.

It took everything I had to sit patiently and wait for her to deliver it to me. When she stood directly in front of me, I looked up. She held the book out, and I gently grasped it with both hands.

When she didn't immediately release it, I met her gaze again. "With this comes great responsibility, Daisy."

I gave her a solemn look. "I understand. I'll treat it and whatever's inside with great respect."

She smiled then. "I know you will. I would suggest though that before you try any advanced spells that you practice them with an experienced witch first. Jocelyn, Aeri, Nicole, or me could help you."

Was I really such a novice? I didn't think so, but apparently, everyone else did. Instead of defending my skills, I nodded. "I'll do that."

My mother resumed her seat and added more iced tea to her glass. "I never expected this path for you. Obviously, there are choices that you're making that I don't agree with, but as before, I'll respect your wishes and do what I can to help you."

I turned my focus to our family's grimoire with a pentagram carved on the cover. The sight of it sent a tingle of awareness racing through me, something unto an awakening, though on a much smaller scale. I opened the front cover and found a list of names that had been written throughout the years, each with different handwriting, and it ended with my mother's.

"You'll want to add yours when the time feels right," she said.

I nodded with reverence.

She studied me. "Don't be in a hurry to rush through everything, either. Take your time. Soak it in. There are likely many spells that are beyond your current capabilities, so tread cautiously and ask for help, okay?"

The Goddess had provided exactly what I needed when I needed it most. I sent my mother a grateful smile, sensing that the recent difficulties in our relationship had eased considerably that afternoon. "Thanks, Mum. I'll take good care of it."

TWELVE

I checked on Nicole before I left my mom's house and found her fast asleep in my old bed. Freya was snuggled against her, and she looked up when I peeked inside. I motioned her forward, and she jumped from the bed.

Quietly, I closed the door behind us and picked up my familiar. I hugged her and kissed her head. "Thank you for watching out for my friend."

Our friend.

I smiled and nodded. "I'd leave you here with her, but I need to see Corey, and you're my security system."

She purred, and I could tell that she liked this new role that she'd taken on. It wasn't until I sat behind the wheel of Gideon's car that I fully realized something that should have been obvious long before then.

I gathered Freya to me and looked into her eyes that sparkled with love. "When I asked how you'd learned to communicate better with me, you'd said it was me, which didn't make a lot of sense because we hadn't been practicing much. But it's not the practice that's opened this world to us, is it? It's that I've been using my magic more."

She butted her head against my chin. *Yes.*

An incredible giddy feeling erupted inside me. "Because of that, everything that comes with my magic is getting stronger. Gideon could speak to you because he's powerful. And now, I'm getting more powerful, too."

Yes.

I shook my head as regret replaced that giddy feeling. "I'm so sorry, Freya. We could have been talking all this time if I wouldn't have turned my back on much of my gift. I always felt I was doing the Goddess's bidding by honoring Mother Earth and being kind to others. I didn't realize there was this whole other side. It's cost us both, hasn't it?"

Her purrs grew louder. *I am yours, and you are mine.*

Sudden moisture in my eyes surprised me. I was lucky that Freya had come to me many years ago. Some weren't so lucky like Vivian who'd only recently found Nooni, even though I wished the man-stealing witch didn't deserve her. Hettie Huber's first familiar had run away years ago, afraid of her werewolf husband. And Nicole had yet to find hers. Some witches never did. "I feel like I've wasted so much time. We could have been talking for years."

She gave me a charming slow blink. *We have.*

Freya was right. "Dang it, lady. Why are you so much smarter than me?"

She leaned forward and licked my chin before she squirmed to be free. When she was seated in the passenger seat, she turned to me. *Corey.*

"That's right. Corey. I need to stop wasting time regretting the past and get on with helping Nicole. Let's do it."

I called his number to see if he was still at Nicole's old house or if he'd gone back to the station. He answered on the second ring and invited me back to the scene of the crime. I didn't particularly want to return to the source of my best friend's pain, but if that's what it took, I'd do it.

He met me and Freya at the front door with interest sparking in his lovely blue eyes. "Did you learn something already?"

I nodded. "Would you mind if we talk out here? There's a lot of negative energy inside, and it bothers me."

He stepped from the house and closed the door behind him. "Sure. I may not have the powers that you do, but honestly, it bothers me, too."

I sent him a look full of gratitude. "You might not have the power, but you still come from a line of witches. It makes sense."

The smile he gave me would have left me speechless years ago. "My mom keeps hinting that I need to find a witch and marry her, that our bloodline would be much stronger if I did."

I gave him an awkward smile, hoping that he wasn't hinting that I should be that person. "If that's what you want, then I wish you luck. I'm sure you'd make a great dad."

He nodded slowly. "Yeah, maybe. Anyway, what do you have for me?"

Freya wanted to be free, so I let her jump from my arms. "It's not a lot, but at this point, I figure anything is good. It took a bit of questioning, but Nicole finally mentioned that Cliff had an estranged sister. Cliff called her Crazy Carly, and he'd told Nicole that she had mental issues. Nicole said his parents were no longer alive, so I figured she's probably the next of kin that you'll want to notify. She did mention a step-dad, too."

He pulled a notebook from his pocket and jotted the information. "Last name? Town where she lives?"

I shook my head. "That's all Nicole knew. She said at some point Cliff and his sister might not have had the same last name, but it's a starting point. Maybe you can connect them through their mother's name on birth certificates?"

A warm smile lit his face. He pulled the phone from his pocket, tapped in a number, and then refocused on me while he talked. "I need you to do a search for Carly Harrison. She might be married by now. She's the sister of homicide victim Cliff Harrison. If that doesn't pan out, then try looking for a connection through his mom if you can find her." He paused for a moment before he spoke again. "Great. Thanks."

He pocketed his phone. "She'll let me know what she finds out."

I sent him a hopeful look. "Could you pass that information along to me? I'd like to let Nicole know if you locate her."

"Sure. Anything else?"

I shrugged. "Just one other thing. Nicole said he didn't have many friends, that he was a boring, stay-at-home kind of guy for the most part. She told me the name of one friend, Roger Evans, but she said she'd never met him, and Cliff had rarely mentioned him. Nicole didn't think that they stayed in close contact. Cliff liked to fish, but he mostly went to work, came home, and had a few beers while he watched sports. He doesn't seem like the type of guy to have many enemies."

Corey closed his notebook and sighed. "That doesn't bode well for Nicole."

The magnitude of her situation didn't escape me, and I released a deep sigh. "I know."

He placed a hand on my upper arm, drawing my attention, and gave it a squeeze. "I'll do everything I can for her, okay?"

I ignored the energy running from his fingers into me and sent him a worried smile. "I appreciate that. Is there anything else you can tell me?"

"Not much at this point. Official cause of death is blunt trauma to the head, likely from the cast iron frying pan that was near the body. The only fingerprints on it were his and Nicole's."

That wasn't what I wanted to hear at all. I focused my gaze off into the distance and reviewed the very little that we knew. "There has to be something we're missing."

He shifted his stance toward the house, drawing my attention. "There is one thing we haven't considered."

I sensed the tension inside him deepening. "What's that?"

He pinned me with a hard look. "That someone might be trying to hurt Nicole instead."

THIRTEEN

When Nicole showed up for work the following day, I was surprised. Luckily, she walked in during a lull in customers, and Aeri and I strode from around the counter to greet her.

We both gave her a big hug, and then headed toward the backroom where we could talk more privately while Nicole stowed her purse.

I studied her features and demeanor as she did. Sadness had dulled her expression and vibrations, which I expected, but I thought I sensed a bit of stubborn determination, too. "I'm so happy to see you today. But if being here gets to be too much, don't worry about leaving early, okay?"

Nicole nodded. Though her eyes grew moist, she didn't shed any tears. "I think keeping busy will help."

Aeri patted her back. "That's what they say. It'll give you something else to think about, and doing normal things will help you feel more normal."

I reached for a clean apron and handed it to her. "Your bruises are gone."

Nicole touched her cheek where Cliff had hit her. "Your mom is an amazing healer." She placed a hand over her heart. "I just wish she could do the same for in here."

Aeri wrapped an arm around her shoulder and squeezed. "I'm afraid time is the only thing that can help with that."

"We'll be here to help you through, too," I added.

Nicole glanced between us. "Thank you for that." Then she shifted her gaze toward the door that linked Meowkins to the Purry Parlor. "I think today is a good day to give the Parlor a thorough cleaning. It's been a while."

I watched her with an uncertain expression. "Are you sure you're up for it?"

She gave me a firm nod. "I am."

The bell above the front door of the café chimed, and Aeri nodded in that direction. "I'll get 'em."

As she strode behind the counter, I followed Nicole inside the Parlor. She glanced about. "The cat beds all need a good washing. The walls, too. I might even deep clean the couch."

I snorted softly. "Whatever helps you feel better."

I'd followed her to ask her the question that had haunted my thoughts since I'd spoken to Corey the previous day. Though once we were alone, I hesitated to say anything that might upset her again. But if I didn't ask and Corey was right, Nicole might be in danger.

She turned toward the closet that held cleaning supplies, and I grabbed her forearm to stop her. She met my gaze with an anxious one of her own. "What is it?"

I scrunched my features into an unhappy expression. "I talked to Corey yesterday after I left you and let him know about Cliff's sister and friend. Then I asked if they had any other leads yet, and he said no."

She dropped her shoulders in despair. "I can't believe this is my life. How is this happening?"

I gave her a commiserating smile. "I wish I could answer that for you. But I can tell you this. First, you're not responsible for his death. That means someone else is, and somewhere, somehow there's a trail that leads to that person. We just need to discover what it is. Corey isn't going to settle on you because you're an easy target. He knows you, believes in your innocence, and he's determined to find justice."

She released a shaky breath. "I know he will. He's a good man. It's just so hard to be where I'm at right now. A break-up would have been bad enough to get over. But Cliff's forever gone, and I couldn't be more uncertain about my future."

I took her hand. "One day at a time. One moment. One second if that's what it takes."

She gave me a sad smile.

"I'm going to do what I can to help Corey, too. Which means I have to ask you something that might make you feel worse."

Her expression grew gloomier.

I kept hold of her hand and focused on sending warm energy through to her. "At the end of our conversation yesterday, Corey said something that I hadn't considered. It's totally bizarre, and I don't see how it could be possible, but I need to ask. He wondered if someone had killed Cliff to hurt you. Obviously, no one knew that you'd broken up that morning so the murderer might have thought killing him would destroy you. Or maybe they wanted to frame you for murder."

She looked at me as if I'd lost my mind. "That's insane. Not only that, but outrageous. You know me. There's not one person who I'd consider an enemy."

I exhaled my frustration. "I know. I can't imagine it, either, but we're grasping for any possible lead there might be. Anything to cast the blame in a different direction."

She shook her head slowly. "That's a dead end. There's no one."

"I didn't think so. Honestly, it bothered me a lot to think someone might be trying to hurt you. The fact that someone entered your home and...yeah. That part is bad enough. I'm really glad you're with my mom now."

Nicole managed a smile. "She's a sweet lady. So kind to me. A little...overbearing."

I chuckled. "She definitely turns into a mother bear if one of her cubs is in danger, and I know she thinks of you as a daughter."

Her smile grew a little bigger.

"Okay, I'll let you get to work in here, and I'll get my butt back out there so that Aeri doesn't think I've completely abandoned her. If you need anything, let me know."

She assured me that she'd be fine, and I headed back to the counter. When I stepped into the main part of Meowkins, I found the man-stealing witch Vivian talking to Aeri. I clenched my jaw. The nerve of her coming into my place.

I strode behind the counter toward Aeri. Vivian must have sensed me or detected motion because she shifted her eyes in my direction. "Oh, hello, Daisy."

The fake friendliness in her voice didn't fool me. "What are you doing here?"

Aeri passed a cup of coffee to her, and she lifted it. "Just came in for a drink." She gave Aeri a pleasant smile before she turned and walked out the door.

I stared after her, suspicion burning in my veins. "What did *she* want?"

Aeri shrugged. "Just coffee, I think."

Through the big picture window, I watched Vivian pass the front of my shop, and then she slowed as she reached Gideon's car that I'd parked along the curb that morning. I usually left that space for customers, but I didn't want to be exposed out in the open any longer than I had to. "No. She saw Gideon's car and thought he might be in here. I don't think I mentioned that she came up to the car the other day and was super surprised to find me behind the wheel instead of Gideon."

Aeri glanced out the front window though Vivian was long gone. "You think she's still after him?"

I snorted. "I don't think. I know. And she'd better watch herself. My mom gave me the family grimoire yesterday, and you never know what kind of spells I might find in there."

Aeri's eyes lit up. "The family grimoire? That's exciting."

I agreed with a nod. "Yeah. I spent several hours last night flipping through pages. Some of those spells are very old and have some odd ingredients like yellow tang. I had to look that one up. It's a bright yellow fish from the waters around Hawaii. They're not cheap, either. There was another with black widow legs."

Aeri shuddered. "I don't want to think about what obtaining those entails."

I lifted my hands in a protective gesture. "Right? Me, either."

I caught movement from the corner of my eye and turned as the door to Meowkins opened. A stylish woman wearing gray slacks and a silky black shirt along with a chunky beaded necklace glanced about the café and then headed toward the counter. Her shoulder-length blond hair was cut in a recent style with her bangs swept to one side. Black glasses accentuated bright green eyes, and when she smiled at me, dimples appeared in her cheeks.

I returned the gesture. "Welcome to Meowkins. What can I get for you?"

She glanced between me and Aeri. "I was told that I could find a woman named Nicole working here. Is that one of you?"

Aeri lifted her brows, but I answered. "Nicole is one of my employees. You are?"

She waved a hand between us. "Oh, I don't want to get her in trouble if now's not a good time. I can wait until she's off work. What time would that be, and I'll come back."

If I hadn't sensed that the woman had a kind soul, I would have made her wait, but she didn't seem as if she'd come with malicious intentions. "Nicole actually manages the cat adoption center here. A few moments of her time are fine."

Truth be told, I'd give Nicole as much time as she needed, but this woman didn't need to know that. I nodded toward the doorway to the Parlor. "Come with me."

She followed me inside, and I went to stand next to Nicole and faced the woman. "This lady, I didn't catch her name, would like a couple of minutes with you."

I sensed Nicole stiffening and tightening the space around her in a protective gesture. "How can I help you?"

The woman slid a sideways glance toward me. "This is personal business. I can wait until you're off work if you need me to."

Nicole shot a quick glance in my direction. "No. Daisy's fine. She's one of my best friends."

The woman gave us a warm smile and jutted out her hand toward Nicole. "Oh, okay. Well, I'm Carly Harrison-White, Cliff's sister."

So much for Corey giving me a heads-up that he'd located her.

Nicole shook her hand, and her demeanor eased. Her intuition wasn't quite as strong as mine when it came to people, but she was still a good judge of others. "I'm Nicole Santoro, Cliff's..."

"Partner," Carly finished for her. "Cliff told me about you. I'm so terribly sorry for your loss."

Nicole widened her eyes. "Cliff talked about us? I was under the impression that you hadn't spoken in years."

A sad look shadowed Carly's expression, and she sighed. "I haven't *seen* him in almost seven years, but I did try to call him on his birthday and Christmas. We'd talk if he'd answer the phone. I'm sorry this is how we had to meet."

Nicole seemed bewildered by the woman. "That's okay. Don't worry about it."

Carly shrugged. "I've been meaning to come out for a while now, but my practice has been so busy, and it's hard to leave patients for too long."

Practice? "Patients?" I asked. "What do you do?"

She dug into her bag and pulled out two business cards, handing one to each of us. "I'm a psychologist. I work mostly with kids and abused women."

I glanced at her card, thinking it looked legitimate, and then to Nicole, who frowned and lifted her gaze to Carly. "But he said you were..."

She snorted and rolled her eyes. "Let me guess. Crazy Carly, right?"

Nicole nodded slowly. "He didn't make you out to sound anything like you are."

"That's my little brother for you. I'm sure he probably told you that we had a rough childhood. There might have been a point when I acted crazy, but that's also what led me to my profession. I want to help kids like us who've reached the point where there doesn't seem to be any hope left."

A pang of sorrow entered my heart. "That's a noble profession."

She nodded. "It is. It can be trying at times, too. Even a little triggering if I'm not careful."

Nicole began to shake her head and didn't stop. "He didn't tell me any of this. Just that he had a psycho sister, and that your parents are dead."

Sorrow weighed on Carly's expression. "Mom's dead. Our father's in prison for the rest of his life, but yes, I'd say he's been dead to us for a long time. My step-dad is still around." She paused to swallow. "And now Cliff is gone, too. I always feared things wouldn't end well for him."

Nicole took a step back. "You need to know that, umm, the police are investigating me."

She gave Nicole a solemn nod. "Yes, I understand that's the case. A nice officer told me that. Sheldon, I think he said was his name."

"Shelton," I corrected.

Carly agreed with a nod. "Yes, Officer Shelton. He was direct with me and said that they can't rule you out yet, but he believes the murderer is still out there. He assured me that they're doing everything they can."

Nicole gave her a grateful but bleak smile. "Thank you for trusting me even when you don't know me."

She lifted a shoulder and let it drop. "Well, I know my brother. I know what kinds of trouble he can get into. And even if you had killed him, it would likely have been in self-defense."

Nicole blanched, and Carly nodded. "He hit you, didn't he? I've worked with enough women to know that expression."

"Just once. Right before he was killed."

Carly stepped forward and placed a consoling hand on Nicole's shoulder. "Well, then, I guess you're dealing with more than grief. Maybe some guilt because he can no longer hurt you. Maybe a little more because you might have wished him dead in the heat of your fight."

Tears sprang to Nicole's eyes and ran down her cheeks as she nodded.

Friskers rushed forward and pawed at Nicole's shoes. Carly bent, picked up the orange tabby, and placed him in her arms. "Here. Take solace from this adorable one." Then she glanced toward me. "Is it alright if I buy us each a coffee or tea and sit with her for a bit?"

I switched my gaze to Nicole, and she nodded. "Of course. Anything that might help her. Drinks are on me. What can I get you?"

Carly smiled. "I saw something about a cat-puccino out there. I'd love to try it."

I sent her a warm smile. "Sounds great."

FOURTEEN

Nicole did end up leaving early that day to spend time with Carly. I wasn't entirely sure I trusted Cliff's sister, but everything she said and her actions seemed to suggest she was genuinely kind and not a deranged woman.

Though it did bother me a little how quickly she'd accepted Nicole's innocence when she knew nothing about her. I supposed Cliff might have said more during one of those phone conversations that he never mentioned to Nicole.

Either way, Nicole and Carly would be having dinner at my mom's that night, and I knew my mom would look out for my friend. Plus, it would be nice to have another witch's opinion of Carly.

As I drove up the canyon to Gideon's and my quaint cottage, I rolled down the windows and inhaled the fresh air still warm from the July sun. Gideon and I hadn't had many relaxing evenings lately, but hopefully we would that night. I missed him, and he was a great sounding board.

The man, even if he was a demon, needed balance in his life, or it would ultimately affect his health. If he wasn't home, I intended to play the concerned partner's role and tell him exactly that in the hopes that he'd come home before dawn.

Luckily, when I pulled into the drive, I was certain I sensed him nearby. One look at Freya's excited face confirmed it. I grabbed my bag and scooped her into my arms. "Looks like we'll all be together for dinner tonight," I said excitedly.

Yessss, Freya said, drawing out the S sound.

I opened the door and was immediately surrounded by the scent of something delicious cooking. Gideon entered the living room from the kitchen holding a glass of white wine. I relaxed my shoulders in relief as I accepted it. "You are the best."

He wrapped his arms around me in a strong hug and placed a fiery kiss on my lips.

I laughed when he released me. "I was hoping you'd get the night off now that your boss is in town."

We both spoke at the same time, laughed, and then he opened his hand to me. "Ladies first."

I grinned, thinking how lucky I was to have him in my life. "I haven't had a chance to talk to you for more than a few minutes for such a long time. I've been worried about Nicole. Cliff's sister is in town, and I'm not sure what to make of her. She's not crazy insane like we expected. At least I don't think she is. And then Corey said something to me the other day, which has me concerned."

He arched his brow. "Corey?"

I chuckled at his needless worry. "He had an interesting opinion."

"Opinion?"

I took his chin in my hand and kissed him. "Would you stop and let me finish?"

He dipped his head, indicating compliance, and I sensed his impatience at doing so.

I'd keep it brief so that he could tell me what was on his mind, too. "Corey wonders if someone might have killed Cliff to hurt Nicole in some way. It seems totally preposterous, but I wondered about Sauron. I know it's a long shot, thinking he would use Nicole to get to me, but we do have a rogue demon around. Or maybe he just thought killing Cliff would be fun."

My question must have derailed his thoughts because he took time to ponder it before answering. "I agree that it's doubtful, but I'll look into it. Demons don't kill just for fun. There would be zero allowance for mercy if that was the case. But I'll send a message to our records department and see if Cliff might have contracted with him."

I narrowed my gaze as I considered what he'd said. "Exactly how persuasive can demons be if they want? Could he have tricked him or coerced him?"

Gideon shook his head. "As I've said before, a person must willingly contract. If Cliff had initially requested to contract and then he'd had second thoughts, a demon might be able to legally tip the scales. But we can't randomly approach people and coerce them into giving up their souls."

I exhaled and nodded. "That's what I thought. And thank you. I'd appreciate it if you'd check for me."

He beamed with pleasure. "Anything for you, my lovely."

I smiled. "What were you going to say?"

Before he could answer, the doorbell rang. I lifted my brows. "Are you expecting someone?"

He sighed. "Yes. I was trying to tell you that I've invited my boss to dinner."

I dropped my jaw in surprise. "Tonight?"

He stepped past me and headed for the front door. "I messaged you earlier, but you didn't respond."

Then a rush of summer air blew into the house as he opened the door. "Antonio. Welcome to our home."

I was half tempted to make a run for the bedroom so that I could change out of my work clothes before his boss saw me, but wild thoughts stole my rationality and galloped circles in my mind, creating a dusty mess.

The next thing I knew, Antonio stood in front of me, giving me a better opportunity to see his features than I'd had at Nicole's house.

He wore his dark hair short and spiky with silver at the temples and sprinkled throughout the stubble along his jaw. Dark, piercing eyes suggested he could read my soul. But laugh lines bracketed his sensual lips, and I sensed that he was a genuinely happy person.

Still, I couldn't deny the darkness that hovered beneath his polished surface.

"Hello, Daisy. It's a pleasure to see you again."

Meeting the powerful demon out on the street with nature's positive forces all around me had been manageable. Having him standing only a few feet away in an enclosed space was entirely different. I swallowed to moisten my throat. "Antonio. We're so glad you could make it."

He held out his hand, and I had no choice but to slip mine into it or appear entirely rude to our guest. I shook it, but when I tried to pull away, he tightened his grip. "I must say you're quite lovely, and the power you carry is...delicious."

My face heated, and I chuckled, trying to bury my awkwardness within it. "Delicious? I think maybe you're just hungry."

His laugh was seductive, and I felt it at my very core. "You're funny, too," he said. "It's a shame that I didn't meet you first."

Gideon sidled up next to Antonio and gave him a hard nudge with his elbow. "Tone down the flirting before you make me think I need to defend what's mine."

I choked on an inhale and pointed down the hall. "If you'll excuse me for a few moments. I just got home from work, and I'm going to change." I took off with wine in hand, retreating to the safety of our bedroom.

I closed the door behind me and sagged against it. I had no idea how to entertain a demon, what to say, how to act. Yes, I lived with one, but Gideon was an entirely different entity. He was sweet and kind, loving and generous.

Antonio on the other hand? He seriously might want to devour me. Or at least my soul. And my magic.

What did one wear to dinner with a powerful demon? I couldn't just throw on a sweater and jeans. Not with them both looking like they'd stepped from the pages of Vogue.

I blew out a deep breath. Men. Was it too much to ask to give a lady a little bit of notice?

I gulped down half the glass of wine and opened my closet. I had nothing, literally nothing that looked decent. Worse, I had a limited amount of time to pull myself together.

In the end, I opted for a black tank dress with a flowy skirt, because one couldn't go wrong with black, right? I slipped on the silver sandals that I'd worn to the Beltane celebration where I'd first danced with Gideon, applied basic makeup, fixed my hair, and added my amazonite and silver pendant that hung on a thick silver chain for luck.

I finished the other half of my wine and left the bedroom.

Antonio was seated on the couch with Gideon in a side chair, both with glasses of wine in their hands. As I entered the room, they stood. Which only made things ten times worse. I held up a hand. "Please don't get up on my account."

But neither of them sat. Gideon smiled at me. "Dinner's ready. Would you like to eat now, or would you prefer another glass of wine first?"

I turned to Antonio. "Let's leave it up to our guest."

He grinned. "Oh, no. I'll let the lady have her choice."

My chest tightened, and I struggled to breathe under the pressure. "Then I say, let's eat. We wouldn't want Antonio any hungrier than he already is."

Antonio laughed again, and Gideon sent me a look that said he approved of my joke. Gideon's boss went all out, extending his elbow to escort me to dinner, even though our table was only a few feet away, not to mention we were in a cozy cottage and not at an elegant affair.

He insisted on holding my chair for me until I was seated and then he took the one on my right side. I frowned at the pretty china and sparkling silverware that sat on the table, certain that it hadn't been in any of my cupboards that morning.

Gideon brought me a fresh wineglass since I'd left the other in the bedroom, and Antonio filled it almost to the top. When Gideon brought the platter of cedar plank salmon and a large bowl of glazed sweet potatoes, my stomach gave an embarrassing rumble. I placed a hand over it, and Antonio laughed. "I see someone else is also looking forward to a delicious meal."

My cheeks must have turned bright red because they felt hot enough to melt an entire mountain of winter snow. I couldn't come up with a quick and clever response, so I just smiled.

Once I had several bites of Gideon's delicious meal in my stomach, my senses began to calm. Although Antonio could be boisterous and he carried a darker version of power in his blood, he was genuinely a nice guy. Though I wouldn't want to meet up in an alley to prove my theory.

It surprised me that most of our conversation was about topics that I might hear at any other dinner table like the latest on the stock market and space travel news.

It wasn't until we'd almost finished Gideon's amazing chocolate-frosted cake with fresh raspberries on top that the conversation turned to magic. And, of course, it had to be my magic that Antonio wanted to discuss.

He lifted his wineglass and studied me. "I hope it's not rude to ask, Daisy, but with a power such as yours, I must know what line you descend from."

I blinked in surprise. "Uh...Aibreann is the oldest ancestor that I'm aware of."

He nodded several times. "Yes, yes. That makes perfect sense. It must be a thrill to know that you're the heir of such a powerful witch."

I raised my brows high. "I wouldn't say that I'm her heir. There are many Summers witches in this area."

He tilted his head and gave me a sly look. "Don't downplay your abilities, Daisy. It isn't flattering to one as pretty as you."

First off, I'd never had anyone like him call me pretty, and secondly, I wasn't downplaying anything. Practically everyone who was close to me had told me that my magic wasn't strong enough.

But before I could swallow the cake I'd eaten and defend myself, Gideon jumped in. "Though Daisy has carried her power all her life, she's only recently begun to understand what she might become."

His statement surprised me, though I couldn't argue that it was likely true.

Antonio tilted his head and regarded me through narrowed eyes. "Is that so?" He sighed with pleasure and looked at Gideon. "To be the one to show her so many things must be...exquisite." He followed his statement with a large bite of cake.

I choked and reached for my wine glass. I wasn't sure if it was because I'd had too much to drink or if it was because Antonio had, but he seemed to be crossing a line. As I drank, I sensed a slight chill coming from Gideon's direction.

He cleared his throat. "Daisy is perfect just how she is, whether she chooses to take her magic to a deeper level or not."

Antonio nodded several times. "Yes, of course. Love knows no bounds."

I appreciated Gideon speaking up for me, but I wasn't about to sit quietly and not say anything. I reached over and placed my hand on top of Gideon's. "It's amazing to be loved for who you are. I'm blessed in that respect. But don't worry. Other than having many years to spend with my loved ones, my deepest desire is to explore my magic until I understand each of its boundaries."

Antonio widened his eyes into large ovals. He held that expression for a moment and then laughed. "By all that's unholy, you are one lucky guy, Gideon. If you two ever decide to bond, man, look out."

I glanced at Gideon, who seemed as dumbstruck as I felt. I chuckled to break the awkwardness. "We're enjoying where we are right now."

Antonio nodded. "Fair enough. Fair enough."

He finished his slice of cake and slid back his chair. "I've probably overstayed my welcome. Thank you both for a fantastic meal. As always Gideon, you're the best chef I know."

Gideon stood and gave him a small bow. "Thank you, sir."

Antonio leaned closer to me and took my fingers. He held my gaze for a long moment and then kissed my hand. "Thank you for the lovely conversation, my dear. I hope to see you soon."

Despite his over-the-top personality, I did find him an interesting and pleasant man. If we met again, I would be much more prepared for his antics. I gave him a warm smile. "I hope so as well."

Gideon walked him to his car, and they remained outside talking for several moments. I wished there was a way that I could overhear them. I had a feeling that what they spoke about was more serious than our dinner conversation.

When Gideon returned to the house, he found me on the couch half-turned so that I could look out the window. He sat next to me. "I apologize if Antonio came across as rude. I've been around him so often that I've forgotten how blunt he can be. Though I've never seen him act quite like that."

I chuckled. "Don't worry about it. He might have been a little forward, but he was charming, too."

He put an arm around me. "Perhaps a little too charming."

I leaned into him. "He seems to think my magic is powerful."

"Ah, now I see why you were able to look past his faults."

I elbowed him in the ribs. "It's better than having everyone tell you that you're weak."

He squeezed me against him. "Your power gives off a false first impression. I was even fooled by it until the other night."

I tilted my head to look up at him. "What does that mean?"

"It means, my lovely, that you have incredible potential. If you want to experience the whole of your power, you'll need to learn to manage and control it."

For some reason, the thought of that frightened me. A shiver raised bumps on my skin. "Will you help me understand it better?"

He smiled. "Of course. I'll do what I can."

I'd never thought my magic was anything special, but apparently, I'd been wrong. Could I really have not known, or had I buried that along with many of my other feelings?

I wasn't sure, but I was about to find out.

FIFTEEN

I'd thought with Antonio in town that Gideon would have more evenings free, but that didn't seem to be the case. So, when my mom and Nicole invited me for dinner the following night, I didn't hesitate to accept. My mom was a fantastic cook and going would give me a good chance to spend time with Nicole without the interruptions from work.

Halfway there, Freya's ears perked up, and she stiffened.

I glanced between her and the road. "What is it?"

She climbed onto the center console and then jumped into the backseat. From there, she hopped up to the top of the seat and peered out the back window.

I shifted my gaze to the rearview mirror and studied the blue sedan behind me. A shorter person with gray hair was behind the wheel and looked nothing like Sauron. "Freya. Talk to me. Is Sauron nearby?"

Not sure.

My pulse jumped. A maybe was bad enough.

The blue car turned, leaving a black bullet bike directly behind me and a white SUV trailing after it. Freya hissed.

"The motorcycle, Freya? Is he on the motorcycle?"

I didn't wait for her to respond before I pushed the button on my phone and asked it to call Gideon.

He answered immediately.

"I think Sauron is following me," I said, knowing that I sounded more panicked than I wanted to. "I'm on my way to my mom's."

"Stay calm," he said in a tone that I envied. "Keep driving. We'll meet you there."

I glanced in the rearview mirror just as the bike turned onto a side street. "Was he on the motorcycle, Freya? Is he back there in a different car?"

No. Not there.

"Not there to begin with, or he's now gone?"

"What is she saying?" Gideon asked.

Freya hesitated and then returned to the front console where she rubbed her head against my arm. *We're safe.*

Stress whooshed out of me in a relieved exhale. "Freya says we're safe now."

When I was almost to the street my mother lived on, we ended the call, and Antonio's shiny silver BMW pulled up close behind me. "Thank you," I whispered to the Goddess.

I parked in the driveway and waited for the men to exit their car before I stepped out with Freya in my arms. Gideon strode straight to me with Antonio not far behind. "Tell me everything."

I worked to separate my thoughts from my emotions. "I'm not entirely sure what happened. I was driving along when Freya alerted me to possible danger. She climbed into the back to look out the window, so I wondered if Sauron might have been following us. There was a sedan that turned, leaving a black motorcycle and a white SUV. Freya had a hard time sensing anything for certain, maybe because we were moving. But then the motorcycle turned, and she said we were okay."

He scratched her head. "Good job, little lady."

I lifted my gaze to Gideon. "So, do you think she was right? Was he there?"

Antonio nodded. "Sauron's been known to drive a black motorcycle. Was the rider wearing a black helmet, too?"

My pulse spiked. "Yes. All black. Black leather jacket, too. I couldn't see anything that made the person distinguishable."

Antonio met Gideon's gaze. "I'll wager that it was him. He must be tracking you somehow."

I frowned, not liking that information one bit. Immediately, my skin began to crawl. "How? A tracking device or something else?"

Gideon wrapped a reassuring arm around me. "I don't think he's obtained a photo of the two of you together, so it's not that. Could be a coincidence in his favor, but I'm suspicious that it's something else."

I shook my head in frustration. "We can't keep living like this, terrified to leave our houses, casting glances over our shoulders all the time. I feel like I should be helping more. Can't you use me for bait and draw him out?"

Gideon tipped my chin upward and gazed at me with his calming eyes. "There's no need to endanger you. You'll be fine. Our precautions are working, and he can't keep this up forever. We've come close several times, but he's shifty. We'll either capture him, or he'll leave town. Trust me, okay?"

I didn't want Sauron to leave town. I wanted him gone forever. But what could I do? "Fine. It doesn't sound like I have a choice."

Antonio tilted his head toward me. "I agree with Gideon. Patience is a virtue that Sauron doesn't possess. He'll slip up sooner than later."

With his arm still around me, Gideon turned me toward my mom's house and walked me to the porch. He placed a soft kiss on my lips and met my gaze. "Try not to worry. Just keep doing what you've been doing. Go in and enjoy an evening with your mom and Nicole. We'll keep an eye on things."

I shook my head to let him know I wasn't happy and reached for the doorknob.

I did my best to leave my fears and frustrations on the porch before I entered my mom's house. No sense in riling up anyone else. Once I was inside, I dropped Freya to the floor and headed toward the kitchen, forcing a smile as I did.

I found them both standing in front of the stove chatting happily. Bless my mom. She was such a good soul and exactly what Nicole needed.

A nearby drawer opened, and a silver spoon flew toward them. I caught it midair, strode the rest of the way to them, and held it out. "Hey guys. It smells delicious in here. What are you cooking?"

Nicole turned to me with her famous smile in place. "Your mom's teaching me her recipe for marinara from scratch."

My mom smiled at me and took the silver spoon. She stirred the contents several times with the wooden spoon that was already in the pot and then used it to dribble some sauce on the spoon from the drawer for a taste. "I don't know. It doesn't seem quite right. Daisy, you tell me."

I leaned my head forward and inhaled the amazing scent while my mom spooned out a small amount for me. "Mmm...it's good. If anything, maybe a touch more basil."

My mom snapped her fingers and pointed to me. "That's it. Needs more basil."

Nicole lifted a jar filled with the crushed herb that my mother grew and dried each year. "How much?"

"Just a pinch," my mom said.

Nicole did as she suggested while my mom stirred and then tasted again. "Perfect. Let it simmer while we get everything else ready, and we'll be good to go."

I enjoyed those moments with two of the most important women in my life. We made a salad with fresh tomatoes from the garden, and my mom pulled the rolls she'd been baking from the oven. I carried a bottle of wine to the table and helped Nicole finish setting it with plates and silverware.

We kept the dinner conversation focused on lighthearted, mundane topics, and everyone seemed to appreciate a chance to relax away from the craziness of the world. After dinner, my mom retired to her sitting room to watch TV, while Nicole and I headed to my former bedroom to chat.

After we'd entered, I closed the door behind us, and Nicole lifted her gaze. "Uh-oh. What's up?"

I snorted. "Just because I don't want my mother to overhear everything that we might say doesn't mean anything is up."

She rolled her eyes. "I know you a little better than that, Daisy Mae Summers."

I grinned and sat on the bed next to her. "Okay, fine. But first, I want to say that it's good to see you doing a little better."

She sighed and nodded. "I'm trying. It's hard not to get sucked under with everything that's going on, but I'm trying to trust the universe to help me."

"I'm glad. You can't control what's happening, and letting it eat you up isn't going to make things any better. How is Cliff's sister?"

Nicole shrugged. "She's doing okay. She's been helping me to feel better, too."

I studied her face. "She doesn't seem to be the crazy person we expected."

"Not even a little. Carly's intelligent and kind. I think she wanted to have a better relationship with Cliff, but he wouldn't let her in."

"That's sad, especially after what she said about their awful childhood."

Nicole grabbed a pillow and clutched it against her stomach. "Very sad. Some of the stuff she told me has helped me to understand why

Cliff was the way he was with me, too. It was unlikely that he ever would have changed."

I shook my head, thinking of the waste of a life cut too short.

She nudged me with her elbow. "Let's talk about you and whatever it is that you don't want your mom to overhear."

I chuckled and slid my family's grimoire from my bag. "I've been looking through this, and there's a spell that might help us figure out who killed Cliff."

She raised her brows high. "Oh, I don't know, Daisy. To accomplish that, the spell must have a fair amount of kick behind it. I'm not sure you're up for that, let alone me."

I frowned and opened to the page that I'd bookmarked. "At least look at it."

Nicole put the pillow aside and slid the heavy book onto her lap. Carefully, she drew her finger down the list of ingredients.

"See? There's nothing overly crazy that's required."

She lifted her gaze to me. "Except a recently plucked gray hair from the oldest crone in the village, along with an incredible amount of magic."

I shrugged. "So, we'll sneak a hair from Jocelyn. Gideon and Antonio both told me I possess strong magic. With you there to help me control it, I think we can do it."

She twisted her features into a frown. "You're making it seem easier than it is, Daisy."

I grabbed her hand and squeezed it. "But it will be worth it, won't it, if we can clear your name? That's the most important thing right now."

Though getting rid of Sauron wasn't far behind.

She gently closed the book and set it aside on the bed. "I think you need to practice more, start with something smaller."

I sighed in irritation. "Like what?"

She gave me a sly smile. "How about you make a batch of brownies completely from scratch, using your magic to do it."

"Brownies? Seriously?"

Her smile grew wider. "Cooking is the same thing as a spell. You put ingredients in, set your expectations, and then use the element of heat to turn your concoction into what you want. People use magic every day and don't even realize it."

I folded my arms. "I was hoping for something a little more unique than brownies. That's a childish lesson."

She lifted a shoulder and let it drop. "How old were you when you stopped practicing on a regular basis?"

I frowned. "It's not fair to use my past against me."

She stood and looked down at me. "I'll make you a deal. You successfully make brownies using only magic, and I'll reconsider that spell. Though we might need another experienced witch besides me."

I stood and grinned. "You have yourself a deal. We can ask Aeri."

SIXTEEN

I managed to measure out sugar, flour, and cocoa powder for the brownies without spilling too much, but cracking eggs was a disaster. After four failed attempts, I begged Nicole to let me do it the old-fashioned way.

She pressed her lips and shook her head.

I groaned. "You're so mean. What difference does it make?"

She curved her lips into a placating smile. "The difference is control. When you have good control over your magic, this will seem easy."

To prove her point, she used her finger to lift an egg, crack the shell against the bowl, and add the egg to the ingredients.

I narrowed my gaze. "Show off."

She laughed, and it was the best sound I'd heard in a while. But I kept that thought to myself in case saying something would send her back into her grief.

Instead, I tried to crack another egg. This time, I managed to get most of it inside the bowl with only one small piece of shell that I captured easily. Good enough, I decided. As it was, I owed my mom half a carton of eggs.

I slowly and carefully added the rest of the ingredients, and I did a pretty good job of it. Twirling my finger to stir the contents became tedious after a few moments.

Nicole shifted in her seat, and I turned to ask if it was always this maddening. Unfortunately, in doing so, I toppled the spoon outside of the bowl, and it left an oozing brown splat on the already messy counter.

I picked up the spoon and placed it back into the bowl. "Oops."

She laughed at me, but I didn't take offense.

When I finally had the batter ready and poured into the pan, Nicole allowed me to place it in the oven with my hands so that I didn't accidentally dump the contents and incur the wrath of her new landlord. I closed the oven door with a satisfied smile from completing my task.

Nicole pointed at the mess I'd made on the counter. "You can use magic to clean that up while they bake."

The woman was ruthless. "I could have that cleaned up in two minutes, if you'd let me."

She shook her head. "But you wouldn't be strengthening your skills then, would you?"

The dishcloth that I'd chosen seemed to have a mind of its own. I had everything I'd spilled piled into one spot, but when I lifted it and tried to fold the contents inside, it flopped back onto the counter and scattered chunks of wet flour. I mentally cursed the darned thing.

My phone rang, and I was grateful for the interruption. I smiled at Nicole who narrowed her eyes, and I pulled the phone from my pocket. Corey.

"Hi, there," I said, trying to sound cheery. I didn't want to ruin Nicole's good mood if it wasn't necessary.

"Daisy, hi." His voice came through deep and sexy. "I have some information I want to share with you. Any chance you can come by the office?"

I couldn't tell him that I was afraid to leave the house because a rogue demon might be lying in wait for me. "It's not a good time right now. I'm at my mom's house with Nicole, and we have brownies in the oven."

"Oh, I love brownies. How about I come to you? I need to speak with Nicole anyway."

Something in my gut told me that letting him come wasn't the best idea, but I didn't know what else to say. "Sure. Come on over."

I finished the call and turned to Nicole. "Corey's on his way. He needs to talk to us."

Nicole's happy mood flipped to dread just like that. "Did he say why?"

I lifted my shoulders and shook my head. "No. Just that he had some information."

The doorbell rang a minute after I pulled the brownies from the oven, and I headed to the front door to answer it. Somehow, my mom had beaten me there and already had the door open with Corey standing in full uniform in front of her. "Corey. It's nice to see you. I hope nothing's wrong."

He spotted me and lifted his chin in my direction. "No, I've come to talk to Daisy." He paused to inhale. "And try some of those brownies."

My mother glanced over her shoulder at me. "Daisy invited you for brownies? How nice. Come on in."

I knew where my mom's mind had headed the moment those words were out of her mouth. She joined us in the kitchen and even went so far as to ask Corey if he'd scoot over a seat. She said the one that he was in made it easier for her to get up and down. Which was a complete bunch of nonsense because the chairs were identical. I had no doubt that she wanted him to sit as close to me as possible.

Of course, Corey complied, and my mom rewarded him with a big glass of milk to go with his dessert.

He bit into the brownie and then pointed at it while he chewed. "So good," he mumbled around a mouthful.

Nicole grinned. "Daisy made them completely from scratch."

He lifted his gaze to me. "I thought you didn't like to cook."

I considered telling him that they likely tasted better because of the heap of magic that had gone into them but decided otherwise. "Baking goodies ranks a bit higher than cooking a meal."

My mom slid the plate of brownies closer to him. "With all the good takeout options we have these days, cooking is overrated anyway. Have another."

He chuckled. "Personally, I like to get in the kitchen and cook when I have a chance, but takeout is nice on the days when I can't."

She snuck a glance at me. "Even better."

I sent her a sarcastic look and then checked my watch. "Oh, look, Mum. It's almost time for your favorite show."

She frowned, glanced at the clock on the stove, and then promptly stood with her brownie plate in hand. "I'll let you all carry on. Good to see you, Corey. Next time Daisy makes brownies, we'll be sure to let you know."

I chuckled to myself. Good to know that her dating reality show topped anything that was going on in my life.

The moment she was out of earshot, I turned to Corey. "You said you have some information."

He wiped his mouth with a napkin. "Yeah. I'm glad you're both here. Saves me a second trip. We tracked down information on Cliff's friend that Nicole mentioned."

Nicole's expression brightened. "Roger Evans?"

He nodded. "Turns out that he has something of a record. Multiple counts of possession of illegal controlled substances with the intent to distribute. Possession of a firearm."

I widened my eyes. "Drugs and guns? Sounds like a bad dude."

"Yep." He shifted toward Nicole. "Also, we found six grams of cocaine in your house."

Her face blanched. "*What?* No. Where?"

He studied her. "Taped to the underside of your nightstand drawer."

Her fear exploded like a bomb. "No. That can't be. Cliff didn't use, and of course, I don't."

He gave her a consoling smile. "We dusted the bag for fingerprints. None were yours, but Cliff's and Roger's were all over it."

Nicole folded her arms across her stomach and leaned forward. "Oh. I just...no. Cliff didn't do drugs. I would have known."

Corey tilted his head to the side. "We found traces in his system."

Her expression crumpled. "There's no way."

She shook her head multiple times. "I can't believe that. Cliff was a boring, middle-aged man who did nothing but fish, drink beer, and watch sports."

Corey exhaled. "Apparently, he gambled on some of those sports."

Nicole looked at him like he'd lost his mind. "Now, you're telling me he had a gambling problem, too? What next? Pornography?"

Corey opened his mouth to speak but ended up sighing. "I'm sorry, Nicole. Sometimes, we don't know the people we love as well as we think we do. He's not the first person to live a dual life."

She kept shaking her head, and her bottom lip quivered. Then she abruptly stood. "I can't listen to this right now. I just can't."

She turned and fled the room.

Corey shifted his gaze to me. "I'm sorry to be the bearer of bad news."

I nodded, thankful that he'd told her while I was around. "I'll make sure she's okay. At least now you have a decent suspect to go after."

"Yeah, that's a good thing."

I thumbed over my shoulder. "I should go check on her."

Corey stood. "Good idea. Hey, care if I take one more of these for the road?"

I shook my head and stood. "Leave one for my mom and take the rest. My mom shouldn't be eating them, and I doubt Nicole will want one now."

"Thanks. I feel guilty bringing bad news and walking out with a bunch of brownies."

I managed a smile then. "Don't. I appreciate everything you're doing to help Nicole. Do you mind locking the door on your way out?"

"No. Of course not." He reached out and placed a warm hand on my shoulder. "You're a good friend, Daisy."

SEVENTEEN

I headed down the hallway to my old room and cautiously pushed open the door. Nicole sat on the bed, leaning against the headboard, with her knees drawn up to her chest. She looked at me when I walked in, and I was surprised to find that she wasn't crying. "Hey" I said softly. "Are you doing okay?"

She nodded, but her sad expression said otherwise.

I approached and sat on the bottom of the bed. "I can't imagine how you must feel, Nic. It's all so unbelievable."

Her eyes grew moist, but she blinked away the tears. "I trusted him. I loved him. Maybe not the forever kind of love, because he wouldn't allow me to get that close to him, but I cared deeply."

"I know you did. You wouldn't have stayed otherwise."

She stared at me with a haunted look in her eyes. "He lied to me, Daisy. Everything about him was a lie."

I wished there was something I could say that would take away her pain. "I'm so sorry. You deserve better."

She gave a sad snort. "Worse, people think I might have killed him. *Me.* The one who feels horrible if I kill a spider."

She was one-hundred percent correct. "I really want to try that spell, Nicole. We can ask Aeri to help us if you think it's necessary. You two alone are smart enough, and if I add my power to yours, it shouldn't be too hard."

Familiar resistance reared its head.

"Come on," I begged. "I made the brownies, and you need to be out from under this dark cloud of suspicion. You deserve time to mourn your loss without everyone talking about you and without the fear of being arrested hanging over your head."

"I don't know, Daisy. Maybe we just need to let the Goddess sort things out."

I shook my head. "Or maybe we can handle this ourselves and let her worry about other things."

Nicole didn't immediately say no, so I pressed my point. "Anything is worth a try if it will help you."

Her gaze flicked between my eyes several times. "Let's ask Aeri what she thinks. If she approves, I'll do it."

We called Aeri together, and when she agreed that it sounded like it was worth trying, Nicole had no choice but to accept our decision.

I was happy that one of my friends could see the value in my idea. "Thanks, Aeri. I'm going to give Jocelyn a call right now and see if she's willing to come over."

Aeri chuckled. "Good luck with that. If you can manage to get a hair, I think that's a good sign that we should go ahead with the spell. Let me know how it goes."

I ended the call and looked at Nicole with excitement building inside me. "This is going to work. You watch."

She shook her head multiple times and then dropped her shoulders in defeat. "Fine. But I'll let you handle Jocelyn. I don't need any more anxiety in my life right now."

"Deal."

I had to ask Jocelyn to come to my mother's house since we didn't dare leave for fear Sauron might be nearby, and luckily, she agreed without questioning why. Which, I admit, did surprise me. I'd think most people would question why they'd been summoned. But maybe she'd had a vision or something that let her know I'd be contacting her. I just hoped her vision or whatever didn't give her a head's up about our ploy.

The sun had begun to set by the time Jocelyn arrived. When I opened the door for her, shadows danced across the lawn, leaving me leery. I quickly ushered her inside and closed the door.

The high priestess of our coven wore her long gray hair in an updo instead of her usual braid, but her flowing skirt, sapphire blue this time, and the numerous bangles on her wrists remained the same. She spotted Nicole standing behind me and opened her arms wide. "Oh, my child. Come here."

Nicole walked into her embrace, and the love and comfort Jocelyn offered her filled the space around us.

After a moment, Jocelyn leaned back and studied Nicole. Then she wiped a tear from her cheek. "I know this is a difficult time for you. But have faith that the Goddess is watching over you. As are the rest of us in the coven. We're here to support you with whatever you need."

Then Jocelyn turned to me and opened her arms for a hug. "Daisy, dear. How have you been? You look well enough."

I leaned in to hug her and tried my best to grab a hair, but the moment was over so fast that I didn't have a chance.

I hadn't seen Jocelyn since she and my mother had tried to intervene on my behalf and save me from my reckless decision to allow Gideon into my life. That hadn't gone over well at all, and I'd avoided the coven since. I was surprised that she hadn't kicked me off the council. "I'm doing great. At least as good as can be expected with what's happening with Nicole."

She nodded her agreement. "That and with having that nasty demon in town."

I sighed in frustration. "You're talking about the man I love."

A sly smile curved her lips and amusement danced in her eyes. "Actually, I was referring to the other one."

I lifted my brows, certain that she couldn't know about Sauron. There was no one to tell her about him. "Antonio?"

She chuckled. "Come now, Daisy. Let's not pretend. That insults us both."

I exhaled and frowned. "You're right. I wasn't aware that you knew about Sauron. But you needn't worry. Gideon and his boss are handling matters."

She gave me an intuitive smile. "Which is why there's demon blood outside your mother's door."

I mentally cursed myself. I should have known that she'd sense it. But there was no keeping the truth from her now. "Yes. To protect her and everyone in this house."

She dipped her head in acknowledgement. "A gallant gesture."

I couldn't tell if she was being facetious or not so I didn't respond. "Would you like some tea? We could sit in the kitchen, or I'm sure my mom wouldn't mind too much if we interrupted her television time."

Jocelyn grinned. "Let's go to the kitchen. Your mother can join us later if she wishes."

I led the way into the cozy kitchen and put a kettle on to boil. Nicole pulled three mugs from the cupboard, and I opened another to reveal my mother's selection of teas. "Anything that you prefer? She has spiced chai, chamomile, hibiscus."

Jocelyn took a seat at the table. "Oh, I'll have the hibiscus. Your mother makes the best blend."

Nicole agreed, so I filled a tea strainer, placed it inside the chipped red polka dot teapot that I loved, and returned to the table to wait for the water to boil. I stood close to Jocelyn, trying to carry on pleasant conversation while searching for the most accessible strand of hair that had escaped her updo. "Hibiscus is my favorite, too. I think she must use extra magic when crafting the blend."

Nicole stared at me with a worried expression that declared we were up to no good. I gave her a wide-eyed smile, hoping she'd take the hint.

I casually placed a hand on Jocelyn's shoulder, making sure my fingers landed on a loose hair. "Would you like a brownie, too? We made them earlier, and there's one left just for you."

Jocelyn turned and looked upward at me. "Sounds wonderful. Thank you."

I smiled, pinched the hair, and turned away.

"Oh!" Jocelyn exclaimed.

I turned toward her. "Are you okay?"

She stared at me for a long moment and then narrowed her gaze. "Give it back."

I flicked a quick glance at Nicole whose expression had turned to one of horror and then looked back to Jocelyn. "I'm sorry. What?"

She shot me a determined look and held out her hand, palm up. "My hair. Give it back."

I was tempted to let it fall to the floor and claim innocence, but I knew Jocelyn would see right through me. Instead, I dropped my shoulders and despondently placed it in her hand.

She closed her fingers. "It's not kind to invite me here under false pretenses and then try to take something that doesn't belong to you."

I dropped into the chair next to her. "I'm sorry. It was just one strand for an important spell."

She snorted. "And you couldn't just ask me?"

I lifted hopeful brows. "Would you have given it to us?"

"Probably not. Do you know how many spells call for the hair of an old crone? If I gave one away every time someone in the coven needed one, I'd be bald."

Nicole sent her a pleading look. "Even if it's for a really good reason?"

Jocelyn slid her gaze to Nicole. "What would that be?"

The kettle shrilled, letting me know the water was ready, but I ignored it. "We want to try a spell that will help us identify Cliff's murderer."

Jocelyn drew her brows into a deep frown. "That sounds like a very difficult spell. To confirm the killer's identity is one thing. To conjure the name of a person when you don't have a clue who it might be? I don't think you have the capability."

I wasn't about to give up that easily. "Aeri, Nicole, and I would be combining our powers."

She seemed to consider my proposition but then shook her head. "Matters of that importance should be left to the Goddess. She understands things that we don't. Not to mention, it could be dangerous for you to invoke such power."

Nicole looked at me with resignation. "She's right, Daisy. It's better that we don't."

I frowned at them both. A little danger was worth saving Nicole's life.

Nicole stood and strode to the stove to get the kettle. She filled the teapot, placed the lid on top, and carried it to the table. "Don't forget, Corey is working on this, too. He just told us that he has a good lead. It's best to let this play out."

I shook my head, not happy with either of them. Then I focused on Jocelyn. "Then *you* do the spell. You're powerful enough."

She sent me a kind smile. "Dearest Daisy, you have much to learn when it comes to Karma. As much as we'd like to change everything in the world to suit our needs, each action we take has consequences. Some good. Some bad. Some aren't known until after the action. I've learned that it's best to focus on putting positive energy out into the world and then let the Goddess take it from there. Everything will work out in the end. You'll see."

Nicole poured tea for each of us. "It's okay, Daisy. Let's let it be for now."

I knew that she didn't like to cause contention, but sometimes that had to be done. Still, I'd let it go, but I wasn't giving up on the idea. If I couldn't get a hair from Jocelyn, then I wondered if one from Mona might work. She and her twin sister Geraldine were the second oldest crones in the coven.

We all fixed our tea and carried on with polite conversation as if we had nothing more to worry about. Jocelyn ate her brownie and counseled me against staying away from the coven for too long. I promised I'd be present for the Lammas ritual.

Before she left, she stopped in to say hello to my mom, and then I saw her to the door.

Nicole was waiting for me when I returned to the kitchen. "It was worth a shot, but don't worry about it, okay? I think getting caught was a sign that we shouldn't try."

I snorted. "No, it was a sign that I wasn't sly enough. I'm not giving up on you, Nicole."

Gratitude shone in her eyes. "I know you're not. I'm not giving up, either. But I don't think this is the way."

Resigned for now, I pulled the phone from my pocket. "I should probably get going. I'm sure you're exhausted, and I am, too."

She nodded, and I called Gideon to let him know that I was ready to go home. When I ended the call, I focused on Nicole. "He's just around the corner. I'm going to head out, and I'll see you tomorrow."

I glanced down at the gray furball sitting not far from my feet. "Come on, Freya."

She followed me to the front door. When I opened it, I was shocked beyond all measure. Jocelyn stood next to her car with one hand on Antonio's cheek, looking at him lovingly. He removed her hand and kissed it.

I stepped out and closed the door harder than I normally would, and they both turned toward me. Jocelyn's expression immediately flipped to one of guilt.

I couldn't believe it.

Gideon waited for me near his car, and I strode toward him. When I reached him, I handed him the bag holding my family's grimoire. "I'll be right back."

Antonio passed me as I walked toward Jocelyn. "Evening, lovely Daisy."

I didn't take my eyes off the high priestess as I responded. "Evening, Antonio."

When I reached Jocelyn, I gave her a look that called her out on her hypocrisy. "Stay away from demons, huh?"

She blinked several times. "There's a difference between you and me, Daisy. You're still a novice who can't control her power."

I shook my head in disagreement and jutted out my hand. "I don't think we're all that different. I'll take a hair as an apology for how you've treated me and Gideon."

She stared at me for several long moments and then plucked one from her head. She set it in my palm and closed my fingers over it. "If you must. We're all allowed our choices in life. But I hope you'll reconsider doing the spell. If not, I hope you'll take great care in what you choose."

I pulled my fist from her hand. "I'm not walking into this blindly or without help, Jocelyn. But I'll allow Nicole to make the final decision."

She gave me a curt nod and headed for the driver's door of her car. I exhaled a weighted breath and made my way back to where Gideon and Antonio stood next to the black Mercedes.

Gideon lifted his brows in concern. "Everything okay?"

I glanced between both men. "As fine as everything can be at this moment."

EIGHTEEN

Nicole seemed to be in a better mood when she came into Meowkins the following morning, but I still wasn't over the fact that Jocelyn had refused to help us. Nor that I had to force her to give me a strand of her hair. I wondered how much of my mom's unfounded fears on the day of their intervention had been spurred by Jocelyn's words.

Stay away from demons. Ha. What a hypocrite.

I waited until the morning rush was over before I gathered my two best friends together, and we huddled in the hallway that led to the backroom.

Nicole and I took turns filling in Aeri on what had happened the previous night. When Aeri learned of Jocelyn's refusal to help, she frowned. "I don't really think it's her choice if we decide to go ahead with the spell or not, do you? Seems she's overstepping her bounds."

Nicole sagged against the wall. "Doesn't matter anyway. She made Daisy return her hair, and I wasn't fully on board to begin with. I think I need to be patient and let the police do their jobs."

Aeri growled her frustration, but I only smiled. "That's not the end of the story," I told Nicole.

She drew her brows together. "It's not?"

I slid the small plastic bag from my pocket and held it up proudly. "I found Jocelyn outside with her hand on Antonio's cheek, looking at him like she'd be happy to do his bidding. I confronted her about how she'd acted when she'd learned I was with Gideon, and I accepted a strand as an apology."

Nicole gasped, but Aeri chuckled. "Good job, Daisy. What did she say?"

I shrugged. "She warned me again that it was a difficult spell, but we already knew that. She said it was ultimately our choice."

Worry filled Nicole's eyes. "I'm still not sure about it, Daisy. It frightens me a little."

Aeri glanced between us and then focused on me. "Do you have your grimoire with you?"

I shook my head. "No, but I took a picture of the spell."

Aeri wiggled her fingers letting me know she wanted to see it. I unlocked my phone, found the picture, and held it out to her. She took my phone and studied it. "Wow. This is really old, isn't it?"

I shifted my stance. "Does that matter? A spell is a spell, right? As long as we have the ingredients, it shouldn't matter."

She slowly shook her head. "No. Shouldn't matter." Then she looked at Nicole. "Your call. Though with the spell needing a freshly plucked hair, I'd say we have twenty-four hours from last night or less to complete it."

Nicole focused on the brown-tile floor for several moments and then shook her head. "I don't want anything bad to happen to you guys if the spell is more powerful than we expect."

I curled my fingers around her wrist and tilted my head to capture her gaze. "Nicole, the worst it can do is steal our energy and not work. You're worth more than a little stress, okay? We're your friends, and we want to do whatever we can to help you."

Aeri took her other hand and squeezed. "Daisy is absolutely right. It's our choice, and we choose to help you. We could, you know, do the spell without you."

She shook her head vehemently. "Don't. If I decide to go ahead with it, I'm going to be there, okay? Promise me."

I nodded reassuringly. "Okay."

Nicole slipped from our grasp and held up her hands. "I just need a little time to think about it. Just give me some time."

She left Aeri and me standing in the hallway and headed back to her sanctuary in the Purry Parlor.

Aeri met my gaze. "Poor lady. She doesn't know what she wants or needs."

I glanced toward the Parlor. "Yeah. She's basically had her life upended, and I'm sure it's terrifying."

Aeri shot me a sarcastic look. "Kind of like having a demon after you?"

I rolled my eyes in exasperation. "I don't even want to think about that this morning. Gideon keeps assuring me that they're closing in on Sauron's hiding places, and I hope he's right."

Aeri gave me a commiserating smile. "Everything seems so surreal right now, doesn't it?"

I agreed wholeheartedly.

The next two hours at Meowkins passed quietly with a slow stream of customers. The day seemed mellow and reflective for us all until Corey walked in. The second that I saw his expression, I knew whatever he had to say wouldn't be good.

He glanced about the café and then sauntered over to Aeri and me at the counter.

I lifted a hand before he could speak. "I don't want to hear it if you have more bad news."

He frowned. "Then I'll talk to Nicole. Is she here?"

I groaned in frustration and shook my head several times. "I'm not letting you talk to her alone. Come on."

Aeri turned to follow. "I'm coming, too."

Nicole looked up from the grooming stand where she had Friskers standing and purring as she brushed him. She looked at Corey, and her expression fell. "What is it?"

Corey walked until he was an arm's length from her. "We found Roger Evans."

She glanced between his eyes. "And?"

His expression darkened, and my stomach dropped. "What? Just say it."

He held Nicole's gaze for a long moment, nodding as he did. "He would be a prime suspect...except he was incarcerated last month."

Nicole wrapped her arms across her stomach, and Aeri moved closer to place a hand on her shoulder.

I dropped into a nearby chair and tilted my face heavenward, wondering why the Goddess chose some of our challenges. I exhaled my frustration and met his gaze again. "So, Nicole is still the prime suspect."

"Am I?" she asked in a scared voice.

Corey glanced between us all. "I'm afraid so, and I'm getting pushback from my supervisor. The county attorney wants us to make an arrest. I'm holding out for as long as I can, but you all might want to say a prayer to your Goddess."

He left us standing in the Purry Parlor with shocked faces. I searched for words that might help but found none.

"I'll do it," Nicole said, breaking the silence. "Let's do the spell."

Aeri studied her. "Are you sure? We don't want to pressure you into anything."

She nodded. "I'm sure. I can't take the stress of all this anymore. I'm going to break. So, if that's going to happen, it might as well end with us having a chance of finding the killer."

I walked toward them and grasped their hands. Energy, pure and simple, flowed between us. "We can do this. I know we can."

NINETEEN

A eri, Nicole, and I decided the safest place for us to cast the spell was in Meowkins. I didn't want to take either of them to the cottage for fear that Sauron might be around and see them. Or if he truly did have a way to watch me, then they might become targets, too.

It might already be too late for Nicole since she lived with my mother, but she was protected while at home and at Meowkins. But there was no need to add Aeri to the mix.

We waited until the end of the working day. I locked the door and flipped the sign to show that we were closed. Aeri and Nicole moved one of the smaller tables to the back of the café where it would be hard for any passersby to peer inside and see us. We each dragged a chair to the table and then sat to formulate our plan.

I opened the picture of the spell on my phone and read through it again. "We already have the crone's hair. It says we'll need sugar to conjure the truth, salt to spit it out, and harmony-times-three candles." I glanced at the others. "Any idea how many that is?"

Aeri lifted her hand. "Nine. Harmony tripled."

Nicole nodded. "Even kitties agree according to an old English proverb. 'A cat has nine lives. For three he plays, for three he strays, and for three he stays.' Nine is a very magical number."

Aeri glanced between us. "Do you want me to run down the street and buy some? It didn't mention a color, did it?"

I looked at the spell and shook my head. "No specific color. Come to think of it, I do have a pack of birthday candles at the desk in the back. Any reason those wouldn't work?"

Nicole shook her head. "Fire is fire. But we'll need something to hold them upright while they're lit."

Aeri glanced toward the pastry case. "We have leftover muffins. Three muffins with three candles each. Harmony."

I chuckled. "Sounds good to me. In fact, since we're using things that are personal to us, I wonder if doing so might fortify our power."

Aeri nodded. "I would say yes, it should."

Nicole visibly shivered. "I'm still nervous about this."

I reached over and took her hand, sending her heartfelt energy. "Don't be. We're safe here. The worst thing that can happen is that we'll feel exhausted for days, or it will fail."

Nicole sighed. "Okay. I'm on board. I really am."

Aeri smiled. "That's good because if you're not, you won't be able to contribute as much power."

She nodded in agreement. "I know. I want this to work. I want answers, and I want to cast suspicion onto the correct person."

"That's right," I added. "Let's give Corey the direction he should be looking. He respects magic and will listen."

Aeri placed her hands on the table and stood. "I'll get the muffins."

Nicole joined her. "I'll get salt and sugar."

"And I'll get the candles and lighter."

Aeri snorted. "We don't need a lighter, Daisy. We have magic."

One of these days, I'd learn to turn to my power first. "Right. Old habits."

The three of us gathered our items and returned to the table. I doled out three bright pink birthday candles to each of us, and we all poked them into the leftover bran muffins from the day. "The nice thing about this is we'll have a snack afterward if we're feeling a little weak."

My friends chuckled.

Nicole dumped the contents of sugar packets on three of the plates that she'd gathered and then sprinkled salt on the opposite side of them. "Remember, the bigger pile is sugar, okay?"

Aeri and I nodded.

I looked at the spell once again and gave them a brief overview of how it was to play out. Then I held out a hand to each of them. "Are we ready?"

They took my hand and each other's, completing the circle. A reverent ambience gathered around us. "We start by lighting the wicks."

I'd always thought I was pretty good at starting a fire, but their candles jumped to life in an instant, while mine took several more.

After they were lit, I cleared my throat and began, knowing we wouldn't have long to complete the spell before the small candles burned out. "Great Goddess, we seek to see. Beyond the shadow and the rain."

We paused for each of us to dip a finger into our sugar piles, and then we placed them on our lips.

Then I continued. "Let light bring forth the truth to me. Reveal the soul who causeth pain."

I wrinkled my nose when the salt hit my tongue and quickly swallowed it. Then I finished. "This we ask, so mote it be."

I met their gazes briefly before I pulled the long gray hair from the plastic bag. With my intentions focused on learning who'd murdered Cliff, I solemnly held the strand over one flame.

It immediately caught fire. A tiny tendril of smoke curled into the air, and I sensed magic swirling around us. But as the fire continued to consume Jocelyn's contribution, I began to worry that the spell hadn't worked.

The flames licked at my fingers, and I opened my mouth to apologize for getting their hopes up, but a great gust of wind stole my words and extinguished each of the candles.

We sat in silence for what seemed like eternity, glancing back and forth between each other, waiting for something to happen. Finally, Aeri spoke. "Did either of you learn the identity?"

Nicole's shoulders slumped. "No. You?"

Before I could respond, a silent bomb seemed to detonate. It sent unseen ripples through the air and slammed me with a force that stole my breath. As I struggled to fill my lungs, a dark form took shape behind Aeri and Nicole.

TWENTY

Sauron appeared, and I gasped as the stone between my breasts grew hot enough to sear my skin. Caterwauls echoed repeatedly from the Purry Parlor, and I wished I'd thought to have Freya join us.

I tried to jump to my feet, but fell to my knees the moment I put weight on my legs. Overwhelming dizziness threatened to steal my consciousness.

I shot a quick glance at my friends to warn them, only to realize Aeri had slumped in her chair. Nicole reached out a hand to me. Then her eyes drooped. She slipped from her chair and landed in a pile on the floor.

I exhaled my horror.

Sauron glanced about the café in confusion. His blond hair seemed mussed, and a sleepy look hovered in his black eyes. Then he focused on me, and a slow smile curved his lips.

He began to laugh, sending the fear of the devil straight into my soul. "This is too perfect. How in Hades did I gain access to your precious café that Gideon had warded so carefully?"

I spoke the only word that came into my mind. *"No."*

He walked toward me, stopping when his bare feet were inches from my legs. Power radiated from him while I struggled to gather my wits.

He nudged me with a toe. "You must have invited me here, dear one. It's the only thing that makes sense."

Had we? The spell was meant to give us a name or vision of the culprit. Not conjure him.

Sauron squatted and regarded me. "Did you invite me, Daisy?"

A slick, oily chill slithered over me, around me, and through me. We couldn't have. That had not been my intention in the least. "Did you murder Cliff Harrison?"

He chuckled and stood. "You brought me here to ask that? I'd thought you might have had a change of heart and were willing to help me with my small request."

"Did you kill him?" I pressed, though my waning energy made my demand sound more like a plea.

He shrugged. "I might have. Though not on purpose, mind you. I'd targeted another. If he'd only done what I'd asked, he'd be around today. Luckily, the Dark One can't hold me accountable for an accident. Really, all things considered, it worked out for the best. I achieved the results I wanted without the consequences."

He winked. "Who knew I'd be so lucky? Perhaps your Goddess is rooting for me."

I struggled to make sense of his words. "An accident?"

He slid a sideways glance toward Nicole. "I needed to distract you. Make you vulnerable, thereby diverting Gideon's attention, which would also leave him vulnerable. How I achieved those results doesn't really matter, does it?"

I brought a shaky palm to my temple. *"You were after Nicole?"*

His laugh chilled me. "Oh, Daisy. Dear, dear Daisy. Delilah to Samson. The consummate Achilles heel. How perfect you are."

He held out a hand to me, but I shook my head and scooted backward as best I could. "You need to leave. Gideon's on his way."

Sauron grinned. "Oh, I know he is. That's what makes this so perfect. When he walks in and finds the massacre of his beloved and her friends, his rationality will cease to be. Thus, giving me exactly what I want."

Incredible fear filled me. Knowing that I might have brought about the deaths of my friends slayed me. I wouldn't be able to live with the guilt. But then I wouldn't be, would I? I would die with them.

This couldn't be the end. Not when I'd just begun to live.

Use me.

The sound of my familiar's voice echoing in my head brought me a glimpse of hope. I wasn't sure how Freya could help, but I opened my heart to her and reveled in the powerful connection. I knew that somewhere inside me strong magic had lain dormant my whole life.

But it was there. I would find a way to access it. This demon would not win. Not as long as I had Freya. Not as long as I drew breath.

The room stabilized, and my vision cleared.

Sauron arched his brow as though he'd sensed the change in me, too. A wicked smile darkened his features, and he lifted a hand. "Go ahead. Try me."

A shiver radiated through me, but I soaked up the momentum from it as well. Then I recognized that I had other sources of energy planted in the walls around me. Love from the cats. Laughter that had been shared by many of the town's residents. The joy my friends and I had radiated whilst making each of our customers' days a little brighter.

I drew it in. All of it.

And then I focused it in Sauron's direction.

The first thing to hit him was one of the muffins from the table.

He snorted a laugh and brushed crumbs from his cheek. "Seriously?"

The inference that my magic might be juvenile was all it took. I inhaled a deep breath and gave him everything I had.

The other muffins flew. A plate caught him squarely in the gut. Another on his forehead, and the third hit him in the throat.

They were little things. Small attacks, but they kept him unfocused.

While he fended off a flying napkin container, I concentrated on Freya. On opening the door to the Purry Parlor. Once released, the cats scrambled, clawed, and screeched.

Finally, Sauron blasted out a spray of power, sending everything scattering. But he never saw the espresso machine coming for the back of his head.

As it sailed silently toward him, I dug deep, tapped into the mother lode of energy, and it exploded from me. With a metallic clunk, Sauron's consciousness and all his energy faded.

The café grew lighter, and the kitties all began to meow. Aeri stirred and so did Nicole. Aeri regarded me with confusion. "Daisy?"

The door of Meowkins flew open, and an enraged Gideon stormed in.

Then he stopped dead in his tracks. His gaze jumped from me to Sauron lying prone on the floor, and then to the disastrous state of my café. *"What the devil happened?"*

Immense satisfaction rushed through me, sweet and strong, and I shrugged. "Things got a little out of hand. But I managed."

Nicole placed a hand on her cheek. "Oh, Daisy. Your café."

I didn't care about that. Everything in Meowkins could be fixed or replaced. My loved ones were safe.

Antonio raced in behind Gideon, his eyes black, and his demeanor ready for battle. He stopped and blinked.

Gideon lifted a hand. "It appears Daisy has done our work for us."

Antonio stared at me for a long moment and then grinned. "Like I said, *delicious* power." He tilted his head toward Gideon. "If you ever tire of this one, give me a call."

Gideon narrowed his eyes. "Why don't you take care of this trash?"

Then he strode the rest of the way to me and pulled me into his arms. "You're incredible, my lovely Daisy."

Emotion welled inside me, and it gathered in the corners of my eyes. "I don't know about that, but at least everyone's safe."

He drew a thumb down my cheek and smiled. "I knew you had it in you all along."

I blinked back tears and grinned. "Thanks."

He gripped my chin and stared into my eyes. "Don't think we're not going to talk about your choices, though. You should have listened to me."

Then he kissed me, and all thoughts of explaining my actions flew away.

EPILOGUE

For the first time ever, I didn't open my shop the following day. Meowkins was a disaster. My friends were too exhausted emotionally and physically to work. Oddly, energy sizzled in my veins. I wasn't sure what had broken open inside me the previous day, but something had.

I felt weirdly exposed driving my own car to my café that morning, and I had to remind myself that the danger had been taken care of. Sauron could no longer hurt anyone.

It had taken some finesse and finagling to allow Corey to *arrest* Sauron for Cliff's murder. Luckily, Corey understood magic and that everything couldn't be explained to suit the average human's purposes.

Gideon and Antonio had restrained Sauron with powerful but invisible holds before Corey had handcuffed him. Then the two demons accompanied Corey and Sauron to the station to give eyewitness statements. They somehow managed to force Sauron to admit to the crime while being videoed.

Then, as Gideon had explained to me that morning, sometime during the night, Sauron committed suicide. He hadn't, of course, but there needed to be a plausible way besides the Dark One coming for him to explain why his soul no longer inhabited his body.

I parked my car, and as I strolled down the sunny sidewalk toward Meowkins carrying my sweet Freya, I sent a prayer of gratitude to the Goddess that I could once again walk freely along the quaint streets of my beautiful old mining town. Sweet Mountain Meadows had certainly seen its share of action and danger, with showdowns in the streets during the silver rush, to an evil demon running amok in modern day.

Good thing most people didn't know about the latter.

As I unlocked the door, I glanced at the sign we'd placed in the window the previous night, stating Meowkins would be closed for minor renovations. I was certain I'd disappointed many who'd expected their daily coffee or tea, but it couldn't be helped.

The moment I stepped inside, the cats in the Parlor began to meow. I visited with them for several minutes, assuring them that all was well. I left Freya in there to play with her friends, and then returned to the café to begin the cleanup process. Gideon and Antonio had helped me straighten tables and chairs and return the espresso machine to its rightful spot while we'd waited for Corey to arrive, so the heavy work was done. But it would take some time to sweep up broken dishes and wipe down the muffin crumbs that had been splattered against the wall.

Then I would do some serious smudging. I couldn't have my coffee shop reeking of a disturbed demon when customers showed up in the morning. They'd never come back.

I pulled the broom from the closet in the backroom and began to sweep. Then I paused and reconsidered my actions. Once again, I'd ignored my magic and that needed to stop.

It took me a few tries to get the broom to move exactly as I wanted, but I grinned when it swept the first pile into a dustpan. Carefully, I moved the dustpan to the large garbage container I'd dragged into the main area of the shop, and I tipped the contents into the trash.

"Woo!" I said to the empty room. The act of sweeping trash was nothing like taking down a demon, but it still brought me great satisfaction.

I was in the midst of directing a rag to wipe down the walls, when I sensed a presence behind me. I whirled and found Jocelyn walking in through the café door that I'd locked. I exhaled a breath full of relief that it was her and not someone dangerous.

Her silver bangles tinkled and her red skirt swished as she approached, glancing about the café as she did. I had no doubt she could easily surmise the gist of what had gone down the day before just by reading the energy signatures in the room. I'd expected to sense some pride in her, but all I found was concern.

I snatched the rag to keep it from cleaning unsupervised. "You could have called or knocked."

Her lips curved into an amused smile. "You're right." And yet, she didn't apologize.

"Sauron is gone."

She nodded. "I hear that your friends are fine and will recover from the stress of the spell."

I narrowed my gaze, wondering where she was headed with the conversation. "They are."

The high priestess took a moment to glance around. "You'll want to smudge."

"I know."

She lifted her chin in acknowledgement.

I'd never tolerated passive aggressive behavior well, and I couldn't now. "Say what you want to say, Jocelyn. You're obviously not proud of my accomplishment."

Irritation flared in her eyes. "What you did was reckless, Daisy."

Her words inflamed the need to defend myself. "We didn't conjure a demon on purpose."

She gave a small shrug. "You didn't know what you were conjuring, did you? That might even be more reckless. Not only with your life, but with your friends' lives, too."

I stared at her for a long moment. "I don't know what you want me to say. Sauron has been dealt with. Nicole is no longer a suspect. I regret putting my friends in danger, but we'd all decided to do the spell together. We live, and we learn."

Jocelyn nodded thoughtfully. "Learn is the keyword there, Daisy. In my opinion, you have much to learn before you ever attempt anything like that again."

She was right. I couldn't deny it. "Those are my intentions, Jocelyn. I want to learn as much as I can about the power inside me. And I want to use it to its fullest."

Her eyelid twitched, but she smiled. "Good. Then I'll expect to see you at the next council meeting and at the Lammas ritual. Perhaps we'll even let you lead it."

I swallowed the anxious feelings her words created and forced a smile. "Great. I'll be there."

She glanced about the café again and then met my gaze. "Don't forget to smudge."

With that, she strolled out of the building seeming cool and collected, but I swore I felt something boiling beneath.

Midlife of the Party, Sweet Mountain Witches, Book Five, is coming in February 2022.

Keep reading for an excerpt from Murder and Moonstones, Book One of the Crystal Cove series, where Gideon makes his first appearance in Book Three. If you've already enjoyed those books, check out the Teas and Temptations Mysteries. I think you'll like them.

Dear Reader:

Thanks for joining me on the journey inside Daisy's world. I hope you enjoyed the story. If you did, please consider leaving a review. It's simple, and it helps me in a profound way to continue to bring you stories you enjoy. All you need to do is:
Return to the purchasing page.
Scroll down to the Customer Review Section.
Look for Review This Product
Click on Write A Customer Review

Your review helps me tremendously, and it can be as simple as a short and sweet, "I liked it".

Also, make sure to sign up for my newsletter and follow me on Amazon for release news of future books and for special offers.

Newsletter signup: www.CindyStark.com
Amazon: https://www.amazon.com/Cindy-Stark/e/B008FT394W

Thank you, very much, and happy reading,
Cindy

Excerpt from Murder and Moonstones
Crystal Cove Mysteries
Book One

Opal Mayland was close. So close.

Less than twenty minutes stood between her and Crystal Cove, Oregon, her childhood home. She'd spent the last six years in Sedona, Arizona, learning her craft at the center of a powerful vortex.

She appreciated the teachers who'd worked with her on spells and potions, since that opportunity didn't exist for her in Crystal Cove, but she'd had enough of the desert heat. The lush green forests full of alders, spruce, and fir trees had called to her soul, and now she was finally back to the Oregon coast.

This morning, she'd woken super early so she could roll into town just past noon. Now, she was so close to home that she could taste the salt on the late springtime air that blew in through the car window.

Opal pressed harder on the accelerator, and the needle on the speedometer crept up. Her sparkly blue Mustang growled as its engine kicked in, and it eased into the next curve as smooth as the surface of a mountain lake.

She smiled, loving the thrill.

Rain speckled the windshield, and she turned on the wipers to whisk it away. She didn't mind. She loved the rain and salty ocean breezes more than just about anything in the world. She'd missed the Pacific Northwest's beauty almost as much as she'd missed her grandfather.

The urge to throw her arms around her grandpa, the town's police chief, was strong, and she hoped he wouldn't lecture her for coming home unannounced. She also hoped he'd learned to keep his share of crazy in check when it came to any kind of paranormal persons other than her. The fact that he'd accidentally married a witch never failed to give Opal a laugh.

The sight of a dark blue police SUV nestled amongst a cluster of trees along the side of the road reined in her thoughts. She flicked her gaze to the speedometer and cringed. Fourteen over the posted limit.

Red and blue lights flashed to life, and she groaned. She didn't need her grandfather to hear that the first thing she'd done on her first day back was to get a speeding ticket. He'd never let her live it down.

She let off the gas and weighed her chances of being able to talk the officer out of giving her a citation. She'd guess fifty-fifty, which wasn't great. But then another option popped into her mind.

What if she tried a redirection spell?

She'd been dying to try it out in the real world, but did she dare? If it worked, it would cause the officer to switch his focus to something else. If it didn't, then she might end up with a citation. So, really, what did she have to lose?

The loud chirp of the officer's siren brought her thoughts to the present and warned she was out of time.

She had to cast the spell now or never.

Do it, her inner voice said. *Do it.*

She glanced in the rearview mirror and released a steadying breath. "See that tree? See that ground? Stop your car and turn around. What you need is not me. Turn away, so mote it be."

The little buzz that she received from casting a successful spell heated her blood. Her mentors had warned not to use magic for selfish reasons too often, lest she invoke Karma to balance her efforts, but this one little thing shouldn't hurt.

She smiled and pressed the accelerator, expecting the officer would pull to the side of the road and then head in the opposite direction.

Seconds passed, and her nerves began to twitch. She continually flicked her gaze between the road ahead and her rearview mirror, but the officer wasn't stopping. In fact, he seemed closer than ever. The SUV's emergency lights remained bright, even with the increased spray of water her tires kicked up. Uncertainty tightened her throat, and she swallowed.

She'd try it again. Maybe she hadn't said something quite right.

"See that tree?" she whispered harsh and fast. "See that ground? Stop your car and turn around. What you need is not me. Turn away, so mote it be."

The officer turned on the siren full blast. It startled her so much that she thought her heart might stop beating.

Sweet mother of pearl.

Her spell hadn't worked, and now the officer was in hot pursuit after *her*. She'd become one of those idiot people her grandfather had told her about, the ones who thought they could somehow evade the law. She needed to pull over before the officer called for backup.

Her pulse thundered in her ears as she signaled, slowed, and came to a stop at the side of the road. The chance of talking her way out of a citation now had dropped significantly.

Then again, maybe she didn't need to worry so much. After all, she was home. As long as her grandfather hadn't switched out the entire police force, chances were good that she'd know the officer. Maybe she could plead for mercy and end up with only a strong lecture about speeding. This was manageable. Not the end of the world.

She exhaled and reined in her fears.

Spatters of rain on the windshield and the side mirror kept her from immediately identifying the tall, obviously male officer who approached. She lowered her window and cast her gaze downward in contrition, prepared to apologize.

"Step out of your car, ma'am."

The fierce authority in his voice surprised her, and she swung her gaze over her shoulder to see him better. The dark-haired officer with gorgeous green eyes placed his hand in warning on the butt of his gun.

Surprised, her breath caught in her throat, and she choked. "No, wait. You don't—"

"I *said*, step out of the car."

His voice was even and clear, and she had no doubt he meant what he said. Her brain emptied of all thoughts, and her hands flew into the air as though they had a mind of their own. The officer opened her door, and she awkwardly swiveled on her seat and stepped out into the light, misty rain.

The officer, perhaps a few years older than her, wore an official Crystal Cove Police Department jacket embroidered with his last name, Keller. Short, midnight hair peeked from beneath his plastic-covered hat. But those intense green eyes intimidated her the most.

Officer Keller glanced beyond her and into the car as though searching for signs that she might be dangerous. "Name?"

She swallowed. "Opal Mayland."

His gaze pierced hers again. "Do you have a driver's license, Ms. Mayland?"

She nodded. "It's in the car. Should I get it?"

"Not until I tell you to."

He scrutinized every inch of her, leaving her feeling vulnerable and exposed. "Are you carrying any weapons, Ms. Mayland?"

Her negative response sounded more like a squeak.

He narrowed his eyes. "Why didn't you stop when I first flashed my lights?"

Oh dear. She widened her eyes into innocent ovals. "I did stop. That's why we're standing here in the rain."

Irritation sparked in his eyes, and she swore they darkened. He obviously did not appreciate her flippant response. "You did *eventually*. From my perspective, it appeared as though you'd attempted to outrun me first."

Her heart thundered in her chest, and she shook her head quickly. "No, sir. I...I panicked."

The white lie fell easily from her lips.

He lifted his brow, indicating he expected more from her in the way of an excuse.

She exhaled a nervous breath. "I know I should have stopped right away, but this crazy thought entered my mind, telling me I needed to hurry and get to a pull-off before I moved out of your way. So, I went faster. Then I realized that you were actually pulling *me* over, not chasing after someone else."

Even to her own ears, her lie sounded utterly ridiculous. She could only imagine what he must be thinking.

He stared, stone-faced. "You expect me to believe that."

Praying that he would do exactly that, she opened her hands, palms up and shrugged. "I have anxieties and don't always react in the most appropriate way."

She watched his face carefully, working hard to keep hers a mask of virtue. Instinctively, she reached out with her senses, trying to discover his hidden emotions but came back with nothing. Perhaps she should tell him who her grandfather was so that she could generate credibility, but her heart warned against it.

He blinked and glanced inside her car again. "I'll take your license and registration now."

"Yes, sir." She snatched her purse from the passenger seat to retrieve her license and then leaned over to grab the registration from the glovebox, all under his watchful eyes. She stood and held out her documents, hoping her friendly smile would ease the tension.

He showed no emotional reaction to her gesture and turned his attention to her driver's license. Then he flicked his gaze back to her. "Opal Mayland from Sedona, Arizona."

She tried a smile once more. "Yes."

He glanced between the license and her face, and then gave a curt nod. "Wait here, please."

With an unhurried swagger, he returned to his vehicle. She sagged against her damp car, and let the rain soothe her stress. Water was the least of her problems. She didn't need magic to know that things with Officer Keller hadn't gone well.

She could already hear a repeat of her grandfather's overused lecture on not driving as though the devil chased her. The thought of it tangled her nerves tighter. She was too old for him to take away her keys, but the disappointment in his eyes would be worse.

The sound of a car door closing drew her attention. Officer Keller sauntered back to her in an annoyingly confident manner. "Here you go, Ms. Mayland. Your record appears clean, with no outstanding warrants."

She could thank the stars for that. "Can I go, then?"

He chuckled. "Do you know how fast you were driving when I clocked you?"

Apparently, he'd accepted her explanation for not stopping, but she wasn't off the hook yet.

She considered his question. If she admitted she was speeding, he'd likely ticket her. Her only option was to continue to play innocent. "Uh...no. I didn't think I was going too fast."

He cleared his throat. "I clocked you at fourteen miles over the speed limit, and that was before you...panicked."

She sighed. "I'm sorry, officer, I didn't mean to speed. I've been driving for days, and I'm so ready to be out of the car. I was focused on my destination and didn't realize how fast I was going until I saw your lights."

Which was mostly true. She *did* like to drive fast, but she *had* been distracted.

He seemed interested in her response. "Are you visiting the area, then?"

Not exactly visiting, but she couldn't say she was a native to Crystal Cove without him asking questions about her family. With it being a small town, eventually he'd learn she was the chief's granddaughter, but hopefully, by then, the incident would have blown over.

"I'm headed to Crystal Cove."

He nodded in appreciation. "It's a beautiful town."

She answered with a smile. "I do love the ocean."

He relaxed his shoulders, giving her hope. "I'm going to do you a favor since you're visiting from Arizona. We wouldn't want you to get the wrong idea about the friendliness of Oregonians."

Thank the stars. He was going to let her off with a warning.

Instead, he held out a clipboard, and her short-lived happiness plummeted. "I've written the ticket for only nine miles over the limit, which should help your pocketbook considerably."

She swallowed her initial sarcastic response about him being too kind and swiped the clipboard from him.

He didn't seem to notice her small display of irritation. "Your signature is not an admittance of guilt. It only notes that you've received the citation. You have the option of appearing in court, or if you prefer to pay for your citation without contesting it, visit the website listed at the bottom."

She signed the paper with an annoyed flourish and shoved the clipboard toward him.

He tore off a copy of the ticket and handed it to her. "Take care out there, Ms. Mayland. Moisture on the roadways can make them slicker than normal."

So, she'd been told. "Yes, sir, Officer Keller."

He'd started to turn but paused when she used his name. He narrowed his eyes and then glanced at the name on his uniform and nodded. "Have a good day."

After he turned away, she rolled her eyes. Cops weren't the only ones who noticed details.

She climbed into her car, her clothes now damp enough to notice, and she sighed. This day was not turning out like she'd hoped at all. Her only wish was that he'd keep silent about the citation or not deem it worthy of conversation. After all, it was only one ticket out of plenty that he'd written.

****

Opal drove exactly the posted speed limit as she passed Crystal Cove's city limit sign and waited for the sense of home to surround her like a warm hug. When it came, her eyes welled with tears. She'd been gone too long and had forgotten exactly how much this town meant to her.

Except for her time in Sedona, she'd lived in the small oceanside village her whole life. Her mother and grandmother were buried in the cemetery at the top of the hill. She'd spent years running the halls of the old Victorian cottage her grandfather owned and countless hours reclaiming her mother's garden. Her best friend, Penelope, who'd been the only one to visit her in Sedona, still lived in the small house overlooking the ocean that had been in Penelope's family for years.

Of course, there were certain unfortunate things about her past years in Crystal Cove that she could never forget, either. Like how she'd walked the beach for days after her old boyfriend had crushed her heart, and how that had led to her asking to attend witch school out of state. Despite the fact that her grandfather had hunted paranormal beings and wasn't keen on any of them living in his town, he'd given his blessing. They'd both shed tears the day she'd left.

She'd grown during her time away, but she'd missed her friends and family. Not to mention the level of pure energy the town received from being sandwiched between the forests and the Pacific Ocean. Energy that could cleanse her spirit of the negativity that she'd received from her unfortunate encounter with that officer. Energy that would give her a sense of renewal and help her to restart her day in a positive way.

She fingered the moonstone pendant that had once been her mother's. It always reminded her that as long as her heart continued to beat, she could start over. And there was no time like the present.

Instead of heading directly to the police station, where she'd likely find her grandfather, she turned on the first street at the edge of town, which led toward the ocean. She'd already intended to complete a small, personal ritual that night in her mother's garden, one that would mark the end of one leg of her journey. Then she could start the next with renewed hope and energy. But why wait?

Her car bumped along the uneven road that paralleled the fresh-water river winding its way to the salty ocean. When she spotted a grassy area, easy to reach from the street, she slowed and stopped alongside the Chemawa River.

She'd learned the power of a renewing ritual from her witch sisters not long after she'd arrived in Sedona. It had helped her to calm her fears about leaving her grandfather alone and helped to bury thoughts of her old boyfriend deep beneath the surface of her memories, where they wouldn't see the light of day.

The ritual was much like a meditation, but one where she invoked the power of the elements to help her. She tore a page from the small notebook she kept in her glovebox and wrote down her intentions and desires, which would focus her energy. Then she folded the paper into her palm and exited the car.

Delightful, addictive power accompanied the breeze rolling in from the ocean. It caressed her skin like a lover's kiss. She paused for a moment to soak it in and let the unseen energy soothe her soul. *This.* This was what she'd missed the most.

Many considered Crystal Cove nothing more than a small, seaside town, but she recognized the forces surging through the air. Strong, beautiful energy, freshly-cleansed by rain. Her grandfather always sensed it, too, but he preferred to think the magic belonged only to the ocean. At least he didn't deny that it was there.

She shut her car door and glanced about to see who else might be in the area. She wanted to focus on her emotions and connecting to nature without being disturbed. A maroon sedan sat parked on the opposite side, but thankfully, no one was around.

She opened the trunk, slid a small black case toward her, and extracted a fireproof ceramic bowl that she'd purchased in a pottery shop in Sedona. The gorgeous piece boasted swirls of red and burgundy and gave her a thrill every time she used it. With as wet as it was in Crystal Cove, it was unlikely she'd catch the grass on fire, but she liked to be careful.

Opal made her way toward the river. She created a path through the ankle-high grasses, down a gentle slope toward the river, and then walked until her senses told her she'd found the perfect spot.

Water flowed past in a lazy fashion, unaware of the cleansing turbulence that waited for it once it reached the vast ocean. She chose an open area amongst the twinberry and ninebark where she could see the river and sank to her knees before falling back on her bottom.

Moisture soaked through her jeans, but she didn't pay it much notice. She was already damp, and one couldn't live in a coastal town in Oregon and expect to stay dry.

She curled her legs to the side of her, placed the ceramic bowl in the grass, and closed her eyes. The sound of passing water calmed her senses. Deep breaths cleared any stress she'd carried from the long drive and allowed her to focus her thoughts.

When she was ready, she placed the paper with her written intentions inside the bowl. With a few whispered words, one corner of the paper caught fire. She cupped her hand along the side of the bowl to protect the swaying flame.

The tender flame grew as it consumed paper, and she held a hand out, allowing the heat to tickle her fingers. "I call to the element of Fire," she whispered.

The fire jumped, died low, and then jumped again, It circled the paper and turned it black as it released her hopes and desires into the universe.

When nothing was left but ashes, she pulled grass from the earth and lifted a pinch of soil. She rubbed the moist dirt between her thumb and forefinger and allowed it to fall into the bowl. "I call to the element of Earth."

She wasn't finished, but already, her soul felt lighter.

She exhaled the remnants of stress and stood, making her way to the edge of the riverbank. She poured the ashes and dirt into one hand and tossed them into the breeze. Some sank to the ground beneath her, while others caught the wind and drifted away into the water. "I call to the element of Air."

Carefully, she bent and scooped cool water into the bowl to wash away any remaining ashes, swirling her fingers around the edge before dumping it out. "I call to the element of Water."

She stood. "Great Goddess, hear my plea. Take negative energy away from me. Transform it into light and love. Grant these things from up above. This I ask, so mote it be."

A sense of calm filled her as she lifted her gaze to the sky. She was home and could be at peace now. The Goddess provided many beautiful things for her to enjoy and be thankful for. The fresh air. The gently flowing river, and—

The sight of something large bobbing in the water startled her, and she inhaled a quick breath. She fully expected to see a log or other debris, but that wasn't what was there at all.

Fear gripped her, and she took several clumsy steps backward. "A body," she said, barely able to breathe. "There's a body in the water."

Murder and Moonstones
Book One, Crystal Cove Mysteries
is available at Amazon.com

BOOK LIST

SWEET MOUNTAIN WITCHES (PG-Rated Fun):
Midlife or Death
For Once in My Midlife
One Midlife to Live
Midlife in the Fast Lane
Midlife of the Party

CRYSTAL COVE COZY MYSTERIES (PG-Rated Fun):
Murder and Moonstones
Brews and Bloodstone
Curses and Carnelian
Killer Kyanite
Rumors and Rose Quartz
Hexes and Hematite

TEAS & TEMPTATIONS COZY MYSTERIES (PG-Rated Fun):
Once Wicked
Twice Hexed
Three Times Charmed
Four Warned
The Fifth Curse
It's All Sixes
Spellbound Seven
Elemental Eight
Nefarious Nine
Hijacked Honeymoon
A Witch Without a Spell

BLACKWATER CANYON RANCH (Western Sexy Romance):
Caleb
Oliver
Justin
Piper
Jesse

ASPEN SERIES (Small Town Sexy Romance):
Wounded (Prequel)
Relentless
Lawless
Cowboys and Angels
Come Back To Me
Surrender
Reckless
Tempted
Crazy One More Time
I'm With You
Breathless

PINECONE VALLEY (Small Town Sexy Romance):
Love Me Again
Love Me Always

RETRIBUTION NOVELS (Sexy Romantic Suspense):
Branded
Hunted
Banished
Hijacked
Betrayed

ARGENT SPRINGS (Small Town Sexy Romance):
Whispers
Secrets

OTHER TITLES:
Moonlight and Margaritas
Sweet Vengeance

ABOUT THE AUTHOR

Award-winning author Cindy Stark lives in a small town shadowed by the Rocky Mountains. She enjoys creating magical mayhem in her witch cozy mysteries, unexpected twists in her emotional romantic suspense, and forever love with hot guys in her sexy contemporary romance stories.

She'd like to think she's the boss of her three adorable and sassy cats, but deep down, she knows she's ruled by kitty overlords. Someday, she hopes to earn enough to open a cat sanctuary where she can save all the kitties and play all day with toe beans and murder mittens.

Connect with her online at:
http://www.CindyStark.com
http://facebook.com/CindyStark19
https://www.goodreads.com/author/show/5895446.Cindy_Stark
https://www.amazon.com/Cindy-Stark/e/B008FT394W

Made in the USA
Monee, IL
23 June 2022